From Tantra
To
Truth

Hard questions ... Real answers

Sanjay Gupta

DEDICATION

To You

ACKNOWLEDGEMENTS

It has taken me more than six battle-filled years to put this manuscript together. I give all my gratitude to all those people who have helped; I am in awe of their generosity and dedication. I have tried to mention the names of all who inspired me to think deeply on the most difficult questions of my life.

In my attempt to keep to the facts, I have cited my sources in footnotes to the best of my ability. To anyone I have missed, my apologies in advance. These will be corrected as soon pointed out.

CONTENTS

Power of Truth

The truth will set you free.

John 8:32

In the beginning, life began with the truth. And the desire and constant search for truth has become the basis of learning—validating experiences and giving reason to studies and investigation. It is this very desire that drives science, education, and art to evolve.

I have spent my life pursuing knowledge and truth, starting in my hometown of Calcutta, India. Although I was always a curious child, my *commitment* to seeking a deeper understanding of my world began at the Calcutta Samaritans Office when I was in my late teens. I found myself in the middle of a group of counsellors and more than two dozen recovering drug addicts and alcoholics. I was introduced as a helper, working toward becoming a volunteer counsellor so I could help some of my dearest friends suffering from substance abuse.

I was always under the impression that addiction was driven by a simple need to wash away physical, mental and emotional pain. Although I had long ago promised my mother to remain sober, I always assumed that when I was financially independent, I would inevitably encounter a pain that I would try to medicate with drugs and alcohol. I was naive. Listening to the stories floating around the room that day revealed a truth that I was not expecting—that addiction is not just a surface level attempt at satisfaction. Addiction was rooted much deeper than I ever thought.

As the session started, people began unearthing their pain, their struggle, their misery. They shared the circumstances that led them to the middle of the ocean of addiction. And they were drowning. Some people felt like their lives were meaningless and empty. Others struggled with suicidal thoughts, desperate to end it all. Together, they bombarded the counsellors with life's most difficult questions, many of which I had being asking myself for years. Questions that had been constantly burning at the back of my mind, never really extinguished.

Why do we suffer? Why is there so much pain in this world? Why are we lonely? Is life worth living? Why did my parents divorce? Why was I abused? Heavier still, age-old questions surfaced again and again: Who created us? What is our purpose in life? Is there life after death?

The anguish in their voices when they asked one particular question pulled at my heartstrings. "If you had to go through what I've gone through, what would you have done? What would you do now?"

My heart was constantly stirring there, burning with a desire to reach out after hearing their stories. Over time, I became an integral part of the team.

Working there, constantly inundated with so much brokenness, I needed to know more. I needed to know that there *was* more. That humankind can still achieve greatness and fulfilment, if only we try hard enough to find it. I was determined to find the true capacity of man. The truth behind what fulfils their needs and stretches their capabilities. I found that I kept returning to three fundamental questions:

1) What is the greatest power man can have?
2) The greatest desire?
3) The greatest treasure?

Thus my dedication to achieving a higher knowledge began. I started reading everything I could lay my hands on that might shed some light: psychology, philosophy, religion, metaphysics, meditation, hypnotism, martial arts, astrology, numerology and many other belief systems.

The search for answers took me on a spiritual journey I could never have anticipated, and I will share my journey with you here, starting from the beginning.

In no way has this book been written to discriminate against any persons, churches, organizations, and/or political parties. I humbly request therefore that you interpret this book in the same manner.

Part One

Genesis

1

There is nothing new under the sun.

Ecclesiastes 1:9

I was born in Calcutta, India, the product of an arranged marriage. My mother was only 12 years old when she married my father, 15 when she had my older brother, and 17 when I came along. We lived with our extended family who ran a business supplying food grains. It wasn't a very warm household. My grandparents ordered my mother and father around no end. My mum was forced to take care of three other children, as well as her own, and do virtually all the housework. My father was no stranger to regular beatings from overbearingly controlling parents, a legacy he would soon inherit. Added to those tensions was the unusual religious atmosphere, with my grandfather dabbling in Kali worship and my grandmother delving deep into black magic and witchcraft. It was, to say the least, not the most functional household.

My mother's relationship with my grandparents was particularly argumentative. When I was around seven, my school choices were being discussed and, again, my mother and grandfather could not agree. My family was kicked out and cut off from the family business. For quite some time, we were essentially nomadic, moving back and forth between the family home and low budget houses—depending on when my grandfather felt like kicking us out again.

When we were in the family home, my grandfather took on the job of my religious instruction. He taught me about Kali, Tantrism, and transcendental meditation. Kali, the Hindu goddess of time and change, was a ferocious slayer of evil. But in her temper, she has a taste for blood and in exchange for a sacrifice, brings wealth to the poor, revenge to the persecuted, and children to the infertile.

He had numerous icons of Kali in a special chamber called the *puja* room or worship room. She had black skin and four arms wielding weapons, her body bedecked with severed arms and a garland of human heads. As a youngster, I visited the Kali temple in Kalighat on numerous occasions. But in spite of my grandfather's devotion and explanations, the experience always scared me.

One time I witnessed something there that stopped me going forever. My aunt was on a mission to gain Kali's favour. A large family party attended the temple together. As we entered, I saw the terrifying Kali idol with her many arms stretched out. A pungent smell of incense wafted around, overwhelming my senses. Suddenly, I heard the desperate bleating of goats. I was told they were a sacrifice. I felt my heart racing. I had never witnessed a sacrifice before.

A priest ushered us all into a small, fenced-in area at the back of the temple, where the sacrifice would take place. Silently, the priest, clad only in a white cloth around his waist, motioned to his assistants to bring two goats forward. The animals' hooves skidded on the bricks as they fought against their captor, but they found precious little purchase and were pulled forward.

In the meantime, the priest had picked up a large curved blade attached to a long pole. He led us all in a Tantric chant as he grasped the goat. Suddenly, he lifted the goat into the air, grotesquely bending the legs back before slamming its body onto the altar, all in one horrific motion. With a second swift move, the blood came down on the goat's neck, and its body was tossed to the other side of the square. The second goat quickly met the same fate, and the frantic bleating was silenced.

When it was over, the family went to the altar, dipped their fingers into the blood, and touched it to their foreheads. I felt sick. It was one of my earliest exposures to the power of religious leaders, and of how our earthly desires could drive us to destruction.

I vowed never to go to the Kali temple again.

*   *   *

During this emotionally taxing childhood, I attended a convent-run elementary school where the nuns called themselves "Daughters of the Cross". They were incredibly strict and conservative, running the place like a prison. The students were treated like sinners in dire need of redemption, as if there was nothing more to us than our wrongdoings. We were conditioned to follow orders without question and swiftly accept the most severe punishments for the smallest mistakes. No escape, no exceptions.

The most common punishment came in the form of a long, slender bamboo cane which was whipped against our backs and palms. The sharp thwack of the cane against skin resonated in the air, instilling terror in all the students. It seemed to me as though the teacher's urge to prove their dominance was restrained only by a prominent pity for the poor souls of the broken students. Pain was handed out more frequently than praise or encouragement. I quickly came to learn that the school had only two rules: firstly, the teacher is always right; secondly, when in doubt, refer to rule one.

Though the heavy silence that lined the corridors of my school tainted my perception of it, I cannot deny that each day was an opportunity to learn valuable life lessons. I consciously made mental notes and eventually had diaries full of quotes, motivational poems, and ways to find meaning in life and the art of living.

At home and school, I was naive and therefore compliant when my devout Hindu mother—my first teacher—taught me that obedience and gratitude were the key to survival. As I journeyed through life, my understanding of this idea evolved, and I eventually learned that *common sense* was key. But as a young, impressionable boy, I respected and obeyed my parents, elders, and above all, my teachers. According to my mother, teachers have a special place in our lives and should always be followed.

She would always use anecdotes and ancient Hindu scriptures to put things into perspective for me. I remember the story about a poet who asks, "If God and your teacher are standing in front of you, whom should you address and admire first?" The "correct" answer was the teacher because they made God known to us. This confused me, as I'd always thought that I was not to bow down to anyone but God. But I took everything my mother taught me as absolute and concrete truth. And why shouldn't I? She was my mother *and* my teacher.

And survival was critical. For many of my elementary school years, I was exposed to leaky roofs, mosquitoes, and all sorts of vermin. Even when we were allowed back into the family home, we were confined to a single bedroom that all four of us had to share. The living conditions, coupled with the increasingly controlling personality of my grandfather, took a serious toll on my dad's mental health. He became less and less able to work, even to provide real parental care. My mother was such a strong person in these times, and I looked up to her so much for it. She picked up where my father was lacking and started teaching the Hindi language to contribute financially. And in the hopes of improving our situation.

*   *   *

One teaching of Hinduism is that a mother essentially takes the place of the Hindu concept of god in this world. We are to love, honour, and cherish her as long as we live. These morals were rooted so deeply in my psyche that the first poem I ever wrote in class was called "Mother".

Mother, you are my goddess,
In this beautiful world,
Your love that cannot be described,
Your sacrifice that cannot be revised.
You will love me even if,
I'll be a dacoit or a thief,
Oh! Goddess Mother,
That I should pray,
May God be with you every night and day.
And all the happiness you gave me alone,
I shall consider them as a loan,
And all the loans I shall try to pay,
All my life with happiness and joy.

It was a reflection of my complete admiration for her. My mother taught me that I was born to be a good person, to make a difference in the world, and to make my family and country proud. She said the most important things for a man to earn were respect, honour, and love. Most importantly, she taught me to respect women. These principles stayed with me into adulthood as I interacted with my peers and friends.

With selflessness drilled into my mind and embedded in my heart, I learned very early in life that everyone saw the world through their own eyes. My grandparents showed this every day, insisting that they were the authority to be obeyed and that our survival was not an essential part of their plan. Everything they did was centred around self-preservation. In the end, family life was all about personal survival.

2

The oldest and strongest emotion of mankind is fear.

H.P. Lovecraft

When I was nine, I had an extremely strict teacher called Mr Wells. He left a great impression on my life, with a cool and shrewd demeanour that always sniffed out the lies and excuses students tried to throw his way. There was no cutting corners with him—it was his way, and his way alone. He expected perfect compliance to his guidelines and anything less would earn intense punishment.

Mr Wells was the kind of teacher who could make a class fall absolutely still and silent the moment he walked into the room. He would inspect each of us as thoroughly as a military sergeant. If anything was even slightly out of order, students would be called to the front of class to be punished. Besides the usual caning and slapping, students had to stand, backs against the wall, knees bent as if sitting on an invisible chair. I remember the throbbing ache that would shoot up and down my legs until, eventually, I was shivering with pain. Most of us cracked within minutes and begged for mercy, but how long we were punished for was completely dependent on his mood. Occasionally, Mr Wells would use pressure points in our bodies to inflict as much pain as possible. No surprise then that my school life was plagued with fear: fear of making mistakes, fear of being wrong, and fear of the ruthless punishments.

The family home was run just as strictly and fearfully. We were whipped for the slightest of blunders, with my father flicking through my schoolwork, each red comment warranting a fresh thrashing. There was no room for discussion or reasoning. Even my uncles, when they came to visit, were quick to take their leather belts to our backs. For a long time, it seemed like my teachers and family had one purpose in raising me: to tame an animal through brutality. This is how they often addressed me, aiming to whip me into shape until I was, by their standards, a "proper human being". With virtually no encouragement or edification from the people around me, life fast became a battle against fear, loneliness, and insecurity. With the exception of my mother, who was herself a victim of the violence at home, I did not have a good impression of authority.

School at least brought me respite through learning about the wider world, and I was an insatiable learner. While Mr Wells's punishments could be severe, he found unique ways of opening up a world of knowledge to us. In our free periods, he would tell us all kinds of stories, and he was a gifted storyteller. Films were his specialty, recounting the stories of Dracula, The Bridge on the River Kwai, and The Great Escape, among others. His ability to bring these stories to life just with the way he spoke left students in a state of admiration and wonder.

The mix of amazement and fearful respect he attracted made a class known as "Question Time" much easier. Question Time allowed students, who would otherwise keep their lips sealed, to ask any questions about sensitive topics like love, sex, smoking, and alcohol. It worked because it was anonymous. Rather than awkwardly voicing our questions on these taboo topics, we could write them down and slip them into a box when no one was around. These classes were the highlight of my week.

Mr Wells was also eminently quotable. There were the usual, yet heavy, clichés like, "If you set your mind to something, don't stop until you've achieved your goals." On the more humorous side, "Any donkey can write a book," and, "Never trust a laughing man or a crying woman."

But one thing he would always say continues to echo in my mind years later: "If we do not stand for something, then we will fall for everything." He drilled such a solid set of morals into the students in such a relatable way that I still look to them today. Persistence in the face of adversity could have been his personal motto. And he taught us that faith in God should always supersede desire to please man. These two morals gave me the tools I needed to survive a challenging world. They are even now buried deep in my heart, seeing me through life's trials and temptations.

Morality was in fact built directly into the school curriculum. Besides the usual subjects, we had an obscure class called Moral Science where we were essentially taught how to be good people. "Love thy neighbor" was a particular favourite. I began to understand that everyone in this world is my neighbour. To make sure we applied it in the real world, we were given a length of thread and were told to tie a knot in it every time we helped someone. We had to present the thread to the class and show how many good deeds we had done and the difference we made. It was a great way to realise how much or how little we did and to look outside of ourselves. As part of our moral science studies, we also performed community service: visiting homes of the elderly, doing their shopping, bringing toys and books to disabled and disadvantaged children, and mentoring younger students in their weaker subjects.

One day, in class, we were told a fable. Two boys had feelings for the same girl. In an attempt to win her over, both boys dressed in their best clothes and went to approach her. She was standing on a footpath, across the road from them. As the boys were about to cross, a blind beggar asked if anyone would help him cross the road.

"I don't want to dirty my hands taking this filthy beggar across the road," responded one boy. "I want to hold the hand of the beautiful girl and ask her to be mine forever." Without saying a word, the second boy took the blind beggar's hand and guided him across the road.

Once they both reached the other side, the first boy audaciously declared, "You saw for yourself how I kept my hands clean to hold yours. You know how handsome I am. I should be yours!"

The girl looked past him and quietly took the hand of the second boy.

This story had a profound impact on me that I have come to appreciate more and more over time. It began to stir my mind to the question about man's greatest treasure.

We were created by God to love and help fellow human beings. Our actions do not go unnoticed. Our value as a person goes beyond looks and intelligence. We are called to radiate the love of Christ, and only after looking outside ourselves to the needs of people around us can we completely realise and fill the void in our hearts with the love of others.

But I hadn't yet learned all of that.

3

Those who stand for nothing fall for everything.

Alexander Hamilton

What is conscience? A whole Moral Science lesson was dedicated to this question as we tried to figure out what exactly dictated our behaviour. It was then that I learned the importance of listening to my inner voice to distinguish between right and wrong. I grew more dependent on my conscience and made every effort to listen to it all the time. I intentionally chose to respond to the little spikes of guilt that surged through my heart when I was doing something wrong. Of course, I didn't always get it right, but I was trying.

Honesty was held in very high regard both at school and at home. It became a keystone in dictating my actions, as there was so much emphasis on severe punishment for liars, cheaters, and thieves. While I did endure my fair share of harsh punishment, I strove for honesty. Like everyone else, I slipped up, made mistakes and found myself twisting the truth here and there. But I persevered and was determined to live as honestly as possible. There was just something about honesty that attracted my respect, goodwill, and trust.

But despite how often we were told to tell the truth, it seemed like no one actually wanted to hear it. People talked about the truth and intellectualised it, and eventually, I realised that everyone has their own interpretation of "truth", which defeats its the purpose. Everyone had moments of weakness, and their truth was often based on their own perceptions, agendas, and needs. I saw how a successful but lying politician could gain all the fame and admiration of the people and perhaps become very wealthy. But the moment they start being honest, they risk all of that. I learned at an early age that dishonesty could break friendships, and hearts. It wasn't worth it to me.

*   *   *

This mishmash of religious instruction I was receiving didn't help much as I tried to navigate morality. School always began with a compulsory morning assembly. We would all gather in the main hall and chant the Lord's Prayer. At such a young age, I didn't understand what it meant to be delivered from evil. But I did know that I wanted to be delivered from fear, loneliness, and insecurity. I was being bullied by both family and schoolmates, and the people I thought were meant to be my safeguard left me terrified and alone. I was young, desperate, and lost. If God is a God of love why are His followers so cruel? And if God cares for me so much, why doesn't He save me from them? I often felt despair.

The school badge was a constant reminder to *Be a light*. It was engraved with a candle with the words written across it. But it baffled me. How was I supposed to be a light when all that was in me was complete and utter darkness? I witnessed my mother praying day and night, fasting practically every other week, and yet still suffering under the tyranny of her in-laws. It honestly seemed like God—whoever that was—was too busy with other things to help her.

*   *   *

My grandfather would sit in front of Kali, goddess of empowerment, for four hours in the morning and another four in the evening every single day doing transcendental meditation, reciting Tantric mantras to gain power and wealth with the help of the spirits. I would watch him in a state of admiration and terror as he went through this daily ritual.

Once, I plucked up the courage to ask him questions about what he deemed the truths of life. He revealed to me that secrets of the occult were told only to those who were worthy. And he could make me worthy. He wanted to make me his successor—as long as I obeyed him without question and proved my worth. His promise kept me obedient and curious. I thought I might finally get the answers to the questions I had been asking my whole life.

My grandfather spoke much about love and goodness as he instructed me in our family religion. And yet, he was one of the most deceitful, heartless, short-tempered men I had ever known. He had a history of violence in the family, including against my dad, whom my grandfather beat whenever he disobeyed orders. But I still respected my grandfather. He seemed to know secrets that would save me from my own darkness, secrets that I was desperate to uncover.

I would question him at every opportunity. I needed to know who created us, what our purpose was in life, and what happens after we die and he gave me something I could hold onto, at least for a while. Hindus perceive *Brahman* as the creator, the life giver, the Lord of Love who created the world through self-projection out of *ananda* (pure delight). He is told to be the Hindu equivalent of the Christian God. Brahman has no beginning or end and is omniscient and ever present, the universal holiness manifested in prayer, priests, and sacrifice.

The soul is referred to as *atama* (breath, wind, air, and spirit). Being new to the depth of Hinduism, I asked my grandfather how he would describe *atama*. His response: "According to the Upanishads, *atama* is formless without blood, shadow, darkness; without wind, ether; not adhesive, not tangible; without smell, taste; eyes, ears, voice or mind; without a name; not ageing, not dying, without fear; immortal, dustless, with nothing before, nothing behind, nothing within. It consumes no one and is consumed by no one. It is the unseen seer, the unheard hearer, the unthought thinker, the unknown knower. That is the infinity in which space is woven and which is interwoven with it."

My brain could not understand any of it. But rather than put me off, my ignorance only drove me to work and study harder to grasp all these concepts. With my grandfather's guidance, I was determined to attain a certain level of transcendental meditation and prayer. I learned all the mantras, all the specific sacred syllables to utter, in the hopes that my sincerity and pure thoughts would invoke supernatural, godly assistance in my life. I worked to achieve complete divine realisation through *tantra*, the ritualistic use of body and mind.

Hindus believe that humans are created when individual souls are separated from the undifferentiated One—Brahman—and that this soul continues to progress through different lives and consciousness. During this process, some souls journey back to Brahman through transformation of the matter (*prakitii*) in which they were hidden. Reuniting with that Oneness is the ultimate goal for each soul, ending the cycle of life and death. As my mentor, my grandfather directed my path to liberation from endless reincarnation, steering me away from obstacles believed to rob man of the knowledge of his True Being. There were six internal enemies that were particularly potent: *Kama* (lust and desire), *Krodha* (anger and hatred), *Lobha* (greed and narrow mindedness), *Moha* (delusory emotional attachment), *Made* or *Ahankara* (pride and stubbornness) and *Matsarya* (envy and vanity). I was instructed to rise higher, achieve more and to achieve the totality that is *dharma* (righteousness), *artha* (wealth), *kaama* (pleasure) and *moksha* (salvation). And this also meant chasing success, respect, and fame in work life.

These conversations with my grandfather were so fascinating, but I was always confused. It was incredibly difficult for me to make sense of it all, regardless of how much I tried. In my heart, I kept asking the same question: If our god is a god of love, then why is there so much pain, so much misery, so much suffering? The theory of reincarnation—that people were paying for their sins through the life and death cycle—partially appeased my curiosity and put a bandage on the gaping wound that this question created in me.

I was encouraged to meditate to open the *chakra* inside me, aiming for full enlightenment. But when I tried to meditate, a terrifying silence would enter my inner self. It was as if I was entering a black hole, my heart threatening to explode and a bright light engulfing me with such a strong force. I felt I was levitating. My body would involuntarily sway, my mind floating in the light. I often sensed darkness eclipse over my head, and fear overwhelmed me. Often, I had the urge to cut my palms and offer my blood to Kali, in front of whom I would meditate. More often than not, I would give into the urge, get into a frenzy, and take a blade to my hand.

It felt to me then that there was no single path to enlightenment; we were all on our journeys alone. Practices that revealed an ultimate truth for my grandfather only obscured God for me. The feeling of loneliness and isolation in me would not abate.

There was some respite from these dark feelings when I was immersed in the arts. I found solace and a kind of soulful freedom in my music classes at school. But literature and the power of words was a revelation to me.

At the age of 14, I was studying Shakespeare's *Julius Caesar*. My first attempt to read it did not go well. It may as well have been in Latin for all I understood. Naturally, most of us, who grew up in non-English-speaking homes, found *Julius Caesar* extremely challenging to comprehend. To appease the teachers, we could only learn the passages by heart without really knowing what we were saying. The archaic text was incredibly difficult. My English teacher insisted that all the students carry a dictionary at all times so we could look up definitions for ourselves rather than question him. Unlike the other teachers, he preferred the hockey stick over the conventional cane to remind us of our lowly station.

After months of exhausting revision and rehearsal, I was eventually able to make a perfect delivery of Shakespeare. It was a big achievement for me personally, and I found that actually, in spite of the challenge—or maybe because of it—I loved speaking in front of people.

I grew to fully appreciate the power of words and the weight behind everything that leaves my mouth. Words have the ability to change lives— for the better *and* for the worse. I know that many of my insecurities as a child stemmed from the constant berating and lack of encouragement from my grandparents and teachers. Even storytelling can have a profound impact on our way of thinking.

For me, the stories my mother told me about courage and bravery became my main source of inspiration. Her words from the Ramayana painted pictures in my mind and illustrated the true gravity of powerful words.

> *You should be ready to sacrifice your life in order to honour your words.*
> *Your words should be your law—whatever you promise should be honoured.*[1].

Two very bold statements that were repeated to me by the most influential people in my life, these quotes resounded in my mind, echoing across time and ringing loud and clear in my head—even now.

---

[1]   A rewording of the proverb, *"Pran jaaye par vachan naa jaaye,"* associated with the 16th-century epic poem and sacred Hindu text *Ramcharitmanas,* by Tulsidas.

Part Two

Exodus

4

Courage is fire and bullying is smoke.

Benjamin Disraeli

As soon as I entered high school, I faced such dramatic changes. Everything was completely different to what I had known. The black and white life and its rules to which I had grown so accustomed didn't seem to apply anymore. The students had the freedom to do as they pleased; uniforms were not strictly regulated, nor were manners or language. My bubble-wrapped ears were roughened by crass words. Skipping or "bunking" class was a regularity that was celebrated.

The majority bullied and humiliated the few decent students—which, sadly, was the only part of high school that felt familiar for me. Any part of me that hoped a new school would maybe change how I felt was immediately crushed when I found I fell into the minority crowd. Once again, I endured perpetual teasing and humiliation from my fellow students, as well as constant peer pressure. My home life had not improved either, and once again I was drowning in a fear so deep, I was glaring down at a black abyss every time I tried to search within myself for a flicker of happiness. Loneliness pushed down on me, forcing me further into myself, allowing insecurity to manifest and control me. Clichéd as it sounds, amidst such a big group of people, I felt completely alone.

One day, the "popular group" approached me and demanded that I skip school with them to go to the cinema. They laughed and mocked my immediate refusal and threatened me. I held firm to my convictions and continued to refuse. The next day, they caught me outside school and pulled me aside. My heart raced as the inevitable punishment drew nearer. I glanced around, trying to search for an escape or a saviour but none came. They pushed me to the floor trying to force me to crawl like a dog in front of everyone. My dignity was all but gone, knees and hands scraped from the rough concrete, but I would not obey them. My eyes burned with the whisper of a tear that I refused to let fall, and I was defiant.

I felt a pull on the back of my neck as I was made to stand. They told me to smoke a cigarette and when I blatantly refused, a mask of anger covered their face. *How dare this kid be so stubborn? How dare he refuse a direct command?* The threats continued and escalated until it became physical. I stood firm. I may have been humiliated, but I held onto my principles for dear life. I would fight to the death for them if I had to. It was all I had left of myself.

My defiance struck them with surprise, and, eventually, they were satisfied with the promise of future punishment. It was only the beginning. They continued to bully me, physically and psychologically. My high school years profoundly tested me. I found myself in the familiar cycle of surviving until the next day, scarcely daring to hope for better.

*   *   *

Loneliness! It's the most desolate word in all human language.
It is capable of hurling the heaviest weights the heart can endure.
It plays no favourites, yields no mercy, refuses all bargains,
Crowds only make it worse, activity simply drives it deeper.
Tears fall from our eyes as groans fall from our lips—but loneliness
The uninvited guest of the soul arrives at dusk and stays for dinner.[2]

During my high school years, my parents, brother, and I were still ostracised from the extended family because of the spat between my mother and grandfather. Though my mother's education was limited, she left the house in the early hours of the morning and returned late at night, still teaching Hindi to support us. For all of my schooling life, I saw very little of her. But my respect elevated as I watched her work so hard for us. I loved her with such boyish admiration, I would come home from school and just stare out the window, waiting for her return. I knew how much she invested into my life. How much sweat and tears she poured into supporting our family. I silently vowed to make her dreams come true when I grew up.

Yet, at the same time, there was a part of me that resented her absence. If she could be such a dedicated and nurturing teacher to so many students—strangers—why couldn't she be that for me? I knew that this feeling was completely irrational. My mum worked because she loved us so much. She threw herself into work to make sure my brother and I had a future. How could I be so selfish? And so my emotions became cyclical. I resented my mother, then I resented myself for resenting her. It's funny, sometimes, how our conscience works. But as I watched the sunset day after day, the door never once opening to my mother's face, resentment

---

[2]   Swindoll, Charles R. (1983): *Growing Strong in the Seasons of Life*. Grand Rapids: Zondervan Publishing.

brewed inside of me, writhing in my gut and manifesting into something bigger. It was a disease for which I had no cure.

At school, the confusion and resentment manifested in other ways. The lessons I had so eagerly learned in my elementary school had suddenly become arbitrary nonsense, redundant even. Personality and charisma were considered incredibly valuable, and a quick, sharp tongue got you further than integrity. A good character was distinguished by wealth and status— regardless of the means to obtain these things. Money, sex, and success were the priorities, principles were forgotten entirely. Friendships were forged for the sake of politics, with fake smiles buying the title of Alpha.

I felt out of place in this new culture, as though I was a leper desperately trying to feign health in the crowd. I managed to make friends with a group of boys from affluent families. In spite of being incredibly rich, they were very accepting of people from other castes and social classes. This privilege showed in their wild lifestyle. I'd often meet up with them and smell the alcohol and tobacco, eyes red from whatever drugs they had been taking. Not the best influence, but I couldn't fault them for lack of heart. They didn't pressure me to participate in any of these activities, nicknaming me "Young Gandhi" for upholding such strong principles. And some of them genuinely cared about me.

I joined them most Saturdays at posh social clubs where they danced, and I mostly sat watching. It was the kind of place where you wouldn't want to be seen dancing without a partner. It amazed me how smooth the words rolled off my friends' tongues as they approached girls, each touch of the face perfectly timed to compliment the sound coming out of their mouths. They were also constantly trying to outsmart one another. No part of me felt even remotely adequate to participate. I didn't have the eloquence or confidence these boys so easily exuded. I didn't know how to act with girls, and the thought of approaching one made my mouth dry.

One day at a friend's house party Pink Floyd's *Time* started playing. The lyrics speak of regret, wasting time away waiting on nothing and doing nothing in the meantime. It wafted into me and settled on my heart. The entire song left me in an existential crisis. It was a crude reminder that every breath takes you one second closer to death. It was the clichéd "Life is short" message but still, it struck me. If you asked teenage me why this song hit me so hard, I doubt I would have been able to answer you. All I knew was that there was a truth embedded in a simple rock song that I wasn't ready to face yet.

Not long after the party, one boy from the group, an arrogant, self-proclaimed karate champion, approached me.

"You know people are talking, right?" he said. "They say that I shouldn't be associating with people like you. You don't know how to talk or walk properly. You don't know how to behave in a civilised society. *I* walk and talk the part. I can dance and fight and be a proper member of the community. My English is much more refined than yours. You with your accent... and me with an American one. You're an insult to all of us."

His words were a dagger reflecting every insecurity and inadequacy I felt. I was numb. The strength of his words hurt more than any sword could. Not knowing how to respond, I simply ran. His words echoed in my mind as I ran further and further. Each step moving to the beat of his words, the sound of my feet creating a distinct *thud* on the ground.

Thud thud. Can't talk.

Thud thud. Can't walk.

I felt completely alone. I was no longer looking down into an internal abyss of self-loathing; I was looking up from inside it. Having been pushed in by the words of that boy, I felt trapped in myself, a dark pit without a flicker of light.

My mind traversed closer and closer towards suicide, skirting its precipitous edges. I considered a number of different methods to find the most efficient one. Diving into a river seemed plausible, so did hanging. But both sounded excruciatingly slow and long. I even thought about swallowing a grenade. It felt like it would fix everything. I didn't know who to turn to or where to seek comfort because the very idea of comfort had escaped me. It just didn't seem possible anymore.

One day, I was with my mother when she looked at me with the softest eyes, her hand reached towards my face. Ever so slightly, she touched my cheek, the simplest act of love and appreciation. A warmth so fleeting yet so powerful radiated from her hand. I never thought such love could be communicated this way but it did. It was as if she had focused every part of herself that loved me into a feasible and tangible substance, transferring that to me in one swift movement. Who would look after her if I ever did the unthinkable?

"Mum? What would you do if I... went away?" I asked. Her composure shifted momentarily as she fumbled with the idea in her head.

"I... would quite honestly die with grief. You and your brother are the greatest gifts God has ever given me. I know you're going to make me proud one day and be a great man." The happiness on her face was genuine, and I fought back tears watching the woman I'd adored my whole life proclaim so much hope for my future.

With that simple exchange, I chose to fight. I wouldn't give up. I loved and respected my mother too much to let her down. I was determined to pull myself out of this rut and help anyone who was going through the same thing. With her support and love, there was no excuse in the way of achieving my goals. I would be the best version of me and find true and absolute happiness.

My hunger for knowledge grew substantially in such a short time. My desire to improve for my mother's sake had lit a fire in me. It was a small flame, but I fed it. I refused to let anybody have the power to humiliate me. I began reading English newspapers daily to learn and practise new words and phrases. I listened to BBC news and programmes on the radio, complementing that with English films that cemented the language in my head. Every spare moment I spent reading motivational books to fuel my fight. The more I read, the more I realised that the intrinsic value of a book did not lie in what the author put in, but what we, the readers, took from it.

I began attending debates and seminars on speaking to hear the experts themselves. I observed the people at each event I attended and mirrored their manners, adopting strategies for engaging people. I steadily added more and more patterns to my social arsenal, refining the public speaker in me and gaining a more comprehensive understanding of the world around me. I knew physical attraction and status were important. But they weren't everything. I was learning how to use my gift of speaking to gain the attention I wanted in my social life.

*   *   *

Enter the Dragon and *Saturday Night Fever* were the "it" films of my generation. Their popularity seeped into mainstream culture, with martial arts and disco-dancing clubs rising up all over the city. I was barely able to afford these luxuries, nor was I technically allowed; my mother was strictly against any manifestation of violence and thought that learning martial arts would encourage gang involvement and criminal behaviour. But I found a martial arts teacher who was willing to teach me at night after his work hours had concluded. As far as my mother knew, I was studying with friends, and I never bothered to correct her. It was difficult to keep a secret from her, and the guilt constantly gnawed at my conscience, but I was so determined to make something of myself, I pushed the guilt away.

In addition to martial arts, I taught myself some dance moves. I wanted to look cool, and it worked. I started getting the positive attention and acceptance I craved. I couldn't help observing people's reactions, noticing how they based their behavior on their first impression of a person. The slight shift in their facial expressions, steering conversations in certain directions. I was constantly discovering new things about how people's minds worked. And about the potency of my own willpower. That little flame was growing bigger, and I was driven to learn ever more.

Soon I found that body language, public speaking, psychology, and personal development were essential ingredients to success. These skills combined into one fundamental quality: charisma. Having wealthy parents, being born with good looks are out of our control. But gaining an understanding of the world and self presenting I could learn. And they proved to be even more important in the long run.

5

Either I will find a way, or I will make one.

Philip Sidney

When I finally started university, I truly entered the dog-eat-dog world. If I had thought high school a challenge, I was naïve. All those "survival of the fittest" clichés proved to be true and relevant. At the core of every animal—including the human animal—is the innate desire to survive. And so, students congregated into groups of likeminded people where they were comfortable. They were split based on their religious, cultural, economic, and political backgrounds.

Manipulation became more intense compared to the games of high school, albeit more subtle. Snide remarks disguised as compliments and strategic affiliations were the norm. I erased my past and plunged head first into the future. When someone tried to hurt or talk down to me, I would retaliate. I had built up an entirely different persona based on the people around me, a tough protective armour. It was all I could do to survive. I needed to know how to talk and fight.

I eventually joined a group of guys with whom I really connected. They came from decent middle class families very different from the students striving after prestige and power. They saw that my daring and tough nature was fueled by good intentions, sincerity, determination, and encouraged me to run for class representative and promised they would support me during the election. I agreed, albeit hesitantly. My whole life up to this point had been plagued with insecurity. I had always been told what to do by very forceful elders. I was an outsider who was now standing beside two very wealthy and well-connected candidates, fighting for one position of influence.

Candidates often used lavish parties, gifts, and luxurious outings to win votes. I did not have the means or the desire to buy votes this way. The opposition threatened me, trying to force me to withdraw. I was surprised by this. It seemed I was a threat in need of elimination which gave me a strange surge of encouragement. I responded in a language of threat they comprehend. My reputation for toughness and martial arts skill preceded me. I never heard threats from him again.

On the day of the vote, the three candidates were required to speak before the votes were cast. I watched each of my two rivals say he would be the best leader. They talked about fun, fame, and fortune. They said they wanted to make the class popular and glamorous.

I was the last speaker, and, as I looked over the crowd of my peers, I vowed to remain honest and maintain integrity. I was not there to speak like a typical politician, throwing out empty promises. I was standing in front of them as an equal, my aim to represent them and make their voices heard. Voting for me was a vote for them. In retrospect, I see now that the funeral speech of Marc Antony in Shakespeare's *Julius Caesar* greatly influenced my words.

My heart thudded as we waited to hear the results. I realised that this was not just a popularity contest. These students meant a lot to me, and I really did want their voices to be heard. I could empathise with their forced silence in the face of authority, and I wanted to change that. I wanted to be in a place of servant leadership—leading my peers by serving them.

The presiding professor beamed out at the crowd as he announced that I, Sanjay Gupta, had been voted in. I walked up to the podium and touched his feet in gratitude. I saw his demeanour change, and the appreciation for this simple act of respect touched his heart. He smiled.

"You're going to be a great man someday, Sanjay," he said. "In all my years at this University, I have never seen a student with such decency and humility that they would show this much respect. You have my blessings, and I wish you all the best for your future."

I couldn't help swelling with pride at these words—though I tried to suppress it. I was glad to be different. I wanted to make a positive change in the community. And this win was my way in.

6

You can ignore reality, but you cannot ignore the consequence of ignoring reality.

Ayn Rand

Once elected I had the power to contribute to real change at the university. I was part of the cultural and welfare team, and I made it my project to lead campaigns on drugs and alcohol awareness. This cause was dear to my heart, not only because of my clear stand against personal use, but also because they were real banes on young lives in India. Unemployment, loneliness, and depression were some of the underlying causes, and I had many friends who were on the road to addiction or else already in its throes. Organising seminars, campaigns, and musical concerts to promote awareness was the least I could do to help my fellow students.

In the midst of this work and study, I had an unexpected encounter. I was attending the 125th anniversary of the founding of St Xavier's College in Calcutta. The guest of honour was none other than Pope John Paul II. It was an unbelievably moving moment to see him in person. He gave a wonderful smile and raised his hands in blessing toward all of us before him. He exuded such warmth, and I left feeling elated.

These years were tough. But I had some amazing opportunities to meet people, to get views from different backgrounds. It was a chance to cultivate empathy and forge long-lasting friendships. And I felt I was making a positive difference for those around me.

*   *   *

Only a small amount of my entire education focused on making money. I was rich in morals and conceptual ideas but the practicality of earning a living was lost on me. My innate perception of prosperity, however, was that money must be earned honestly and shared with the needy.

As a youngster my allowance was limited to 10p a day, just enough to buy a small packet of peanuts or two cookies. One day, I was eating an apple during the lunch break when I saw an orphan boy watching me. I had finished the apple and threw away the core. The boy asked what I had been eating. I was amazed to see him rummage through the bin and eat the remains of the apple core. My heart broke at this desperate grab for sustenance, and I made it a point to bring extra food with my 10p, ready to be distributed to the other orphan kids that didn't have enough. To this day, I now eat the entirety of the apple, leaving only the seeds for rubbish.

At university, ironically, I was studying commerce more as a fall back than anything else—I had no idea which career I'd pursue after I graduated. In the middle of my university life, I began to think seriously about joining the army. The thought of it promised my young mind honour, adventure, and—dare I say—excitement. It seemed like a noble profession—self-sacrifice for the sake of my home country that I loved. The only thing that brought reluctance into my otherwise sure heart was the thought of leaving my mother alone. And for the moment, it was enough to stop me from going down that path.

I studied accountancy instead—not exactly the honour, adventure, and excitement I was seeking. But as we learned the ins and outs of business, I found I really enjoyed these subjects. Economics in particular piqued my interest, mainly because I learned the finite amount of resources available to the unlimited wants of man. It was the basic principle of supply and demand that, once I had formally learned it, seemed to apply to so many facets in life. The more we have, the less we need, but the moment we have little of something, we suddenly desire more of it. I learned the differences between necessity, comfort, and luxury.

At the age of 19, I was beginning to lean towards a more self-sufficient lifestyle. I began privately tutoring to support myself and contribute to my family's expenses. My father had serious health issues, shifting family responsibility onto my shoulders that were barely big enough to carry them. I took care of my mother and paid for my own education. It was exhausting and difficult, a crude way to learn responsibility. I had no support from any of the rest of the family, and I couldn't help comparing myself to my fellow students.

They were so fortunate, and they weren't even slightly aware of it. They came from strong and wealthy families, with businesses to support them and a future already prepared for them. I so wished I had someone to turn to. It was a difficult period in my life, testing every moral obligation I had developed over the years. But my mother's strong influence prevailed. I never compromised on those principles she had instilled in me long ago. I still shared with the less fortunate and, thankfully, I still loved, gave, and cared. I sought success, but I was determined to remain sincere in the face of it all.

My desire for financial and personal success was also strong. But the "get rich quick" scheme never appealed to me. I was incredibly wary of it because of the dishonesty it often brought. But I needed funds and connections to start me off in the business world. I found some business assignments through a friend, selling water-based rust paint for cars. I worked hard for him. "Don't come back until you have achieved your goals" became my motto, and I managed to introduce the product to some big companies—even to the police and the army. Things were going well, and I felt that I was finally getting somewhere, becoming financially secure.

But then I learned another, very painful, lesson. People will take advantage of you if they can, taking what they want from you before throwing you out. The friend I trusted let me forge good relationships with these companies, and then cut me out of the picture to deal with them directly. I never got the commission I was promised and rightfully earned. My automatic reaction was to retreat, withdraw into myself and into the familiar pool of insecurity, loneliness, and fear. It terrified me how easy it was for me to fall back into that discomfort. I had hoped these feeling had left, but there they were, just hidden from my immediate awareness, ready to emerge when my confidence was even slightly tested, tendrils of dread invading my heart without a moment's notice.

I quickly lost my taste for the sales business, finding it soulless from then on. I vowed that I wouldn't work under anyone. Nor would I dare lie, cheat, or manipulate people for my own benefit.

*   *   *

After two years of study, I switched to a different university, studying English, history, and political science. But I was getting more and more disillusioned with life again. By age 21, I was quite cynical, bitter and suspicious. The more I learned about the world, the less I liked it. It pushed any sense of theism out of me. God was now an imaginary being to me, created by man to support weakness, a scapegoat to blame for our laziness and misfortune. Religion was a business for the talented who had the intelligence to fool others.

I eventually came across the famous book, Mario Puzo's *The Godfather*, the story of a man so disillusioned by the world's injustice, crime, and corruption that he builds his own empire to give his loved ones protection, and power. Unlikely though it would appear seeing as it's about a crime syndicate, the book seemed to hold all the answers to my questions—my version of the gospel, if you will. It emulated my internal thoughts "that the world is so hard, a man must have two fathers to look after him."[3] Of course, in the book, it meant having a godfather. But for me, it explained people's yearning for a higher power. I thought about my own father's inability to care for his family. I saw that the world was a hard place to live in, and having a god, fake or not, brought comfort to many.

This character, Don Corleone, the Godfather, was speaking from such a real human perspective, as if knowingly addressing my emotions. He was a man of principles, flawed though they were. He was ready to protect and sacrifice for the people he loved, a man of integrity of a sort, and wisdom, who valued his family. He existed for himself and for the people he loved. Not for God. I found a lot of inspiration in this book for my behavior with other people.

*　　*　　*

I loved my friends more than I did my family at the time and was willing to do anything they needed. I felt trusted and respected for my integrity and principles. I never had any problems accepting and befriending

---

[3]　　Puzo, Mario (2009): *The Godfather*. London: The Random House Group (Original work published 1969)

people from different classes, religions, or backgrounds. All I needed was honesty, loyalty, and respect. Making friends, and eventually family, of strangers came naturally to me.

I used to practise martial arts every morning in a nearby park. I noticed kids in the area copying me from afar so I asked them to join me. Eventually, the group grew to about sixty children, and I was teaching them martial arts. The kids ranged from different social statuses, and I was honoured to be their guide and mentor. Their constant devotion and dedication humbled me as a teacher. Who was teaching whom?

Once, my barber was telling me about his poor background and his desire to learn English to better his future. This inspired me to expand my teaching and take on another group of evening students to teach them English. Being in these environments left me feeling enriched and happy. There is something very special, almost magical, about this type of relationship, a genuine respect between teacher and student. It couldn't have been more different from my own schooling.

A good friend of mine knew about these lessons and connected me to the Lions Club in Calcutta. They paid me very well to teach effective communication to rich and influential people. They were the game changers, the movers, the world shakers of Calcutta and were out to make a difference in society. And suddenly they were learning from me. It was a strange change!

From poor children picking up some martial arts moves to executives learning how to diplomatically communicate, so many of my students seemed full of joy. For me, helping these people was my euphoria. It gave me a sense of purpose and satisfaction I wasn't familiar with. I treasured these experiences and the feelings of self-worth they imbued in me.

Part Three

Judges

7

God moves in mysterious ways.

William Cowper

One winter weekend, when I was 22, a friend of mine invited me to a Christian camp his church was hosting. I went along with him because I expected it to be dominated by games and socialising. Once we arrived, however, I was surprised and disappointed to find that it was a Bible camp for young adults. I was so adamant about turning away from God that I made it my mission to take people with me. My aim for the duration of the camp was to reveal my truth to these people, to prove that they were escapists, the very hypocrites I had begun to loathe for hiding behind an imaginary God-shaped shield to hide their own falseness.

From day one, I made my intentions very clear. I proudly boasted of what I thought at the time was my enlightened state of mind. My atheism was my identifier, and I made sure everybody knew it. When the first preacher began speaking, I was prepared. She was a doctor, telling the congregation her testimony. She stepped onto the platform and spoke bravely, telling us how she left her fiancé because he was not Christian and unwilling to convert. Something within me sparked, and I immediately pushed my hand into the air. Shocked, she stared at me.

"Yes...?" she asked, puzzled. I interpreted her shock as hesitation and therefore insecurity. I smirked at her weakness.

"How come a God of love was so petty not to accept someone born in a different faith?" I asked haughtily.

Her reaction made it clear that such a question was unprecedented and not expected in this kind of setting. That made me even happier.

When she composed herself, she replied, "You don't understand because you don't have a personal relationship with God. But the moment that you experience the true depth of His love and taste what He offers is the moment you stop living for yourself and start living for Him. Was it hard to leave the man I was engaged to? Yes. But my love for God was much stronger, and I was—am—willing to honour that until the end. To put it in perspective, imagine my fiancé and I standing on the floor together when I meet with my Father, and He lifts me higher to stand on a table. My fiancé is still down, and as hard as I try to pull him up with me, he won't commit, and it's more likely that he will pull me back down. I wasn't willing to risk that."

"Do you know—or even care—what state he might be in now?" I responded. Her response had recalled what I had admired about the Godfather—he lives for himself, not for God. This woman proudly lived for God, but at a seemingly terrible cost. "What must be going through his heart and mind?" I turned to the congregation, opening the question to everyone who was now listening intently, the air thick with nervous tension. "I don't understand any of this," I went on. "What I'm hearing is that you have a God who is apparently an ever-loving God but allows you to break somebody's heart like that and cause him so much pain. How does that make sense? I just don't understand."

I glanced back at the doctor and saw that tears were rolling down her cheeks. I took that as a sign of her defeat, but I felt unexpectedly deflated. I sat back down, feeling both confused and victorious.

Later that afternoon, however, she approached me. She told me ever so politely that I had stirred something in her heart that told her she needed to go see her ex-fiancé soon and see how he was doing. It was bizarre. Here I was, a boy who had just humiliated her and put her on the spot in front of an entire camp, and she was telling me how my words had inspired her to reach out. I was taken aback by this attitude and grew more and more confused.

For the next two days, I persisted with my antagonism toward these believers. Any time a preacher stood before the group, I attacked them with more questions. With anger and frustration fueling my words, I was difficult to ignore. People noticed, and I knew it. One person approached me, saying there was a group who were constantly praying for me. I laughed at the thought. What a strange solution. How would prayer help anything?

On the third day, one of the speakers pulled me aside after lunch and asked to take a walk. Here we go, I thought. I agreed, thinking I knew exactly what this would be about. I was actually excited about it. Despite what would surely be his attempt to talk at me until I became a Christian, I would take this opportunity to reveal *my* truth to him. I thought it would be easy to show him that God didn't exist with my knowledge of the world and the overwhelming evidence against Him.

I was expecting him to start lecturing me on the Bible. I was surprised to hear him simply say, "So tell me about yourself." His face showed genuine interest in me. I went ahead and told him all about my life.

I told him about my Hindu background— it was an extremely ancient religion, with origins far older than Christianity. I confined that my grandfather was a great Sanskrit scholar, well-versed in the spiritual side of the world, and yet I could still confidently say there was no God. I told him about my grandfather's cruelty and unmatched selfishness, a direct contradiction to my sweet, devout mother who prayed constantly to the gods but her prayers were never answered. My voice cracked as I spoke about my mother, and what had started as a discourse on my superiority in spiritual knowledge took an unexpectedly emotional turn. I found words tumbling out of my mouth, and I recalled a particular story I hadn't thought about for years.

On a pilgrimage to the Himalayan Kedarnath Temple with my mother, we walked through 14km of snow-capped mountains to reach the shrine dedicated to Lord Shiva. Where my mother took an apparent holy dip in the icy water flowing from the mountains. It was meant to bring blessings on her life. That very night, she fell very ill. Her temperature sky-rocketed, and with no doctors nearby the possibility of losing her became scarily real. I hated God in this moment. There was no God. If there was, he wouldn't make my mother suffer like this after she showed her devotion. The whole thing was a con created by elders and leaders to gain wealth and power. The whole episode sickened me.

The more I spoke, the more I realised how raw I was being with this man I barely knew. I was painfully honest and vulnerable, yet he continued to listen. I talked about my convent school, further evidence for me of God's nonexistence, with prayer used as a desperate grab for good grades that never came, and His people ill-treating students. No, God was unreal. A man-made creation to appease us in the midst of broken dreams and laziness. Removing all responsibility from ourselves and trading it in for a cross because we were too afraid to consider death.

"Richard Bach once said," I began, excited now because I felt I was converting him to my side, "if you practise being fictional for a while, you will understand that fictional characters are sometimes more real than people with heartbeats and bodies."[4]

I thought I had unraveled his entire belief system. "In my opinion," I continued, "true love and friendship is greater than any religion or so-called God. Some of my closest friends are drug addicts and alcoholics, but I love and care for them because of their heart and not their habit. Because they're honest., they know they can't face the heartaches of a hypocritical society and gladly take refuge in chemicals rather than hiding behind the curtain of religion. When you love somebody—platonic or otherwise—you become loyal, sacrificial and protective. When the people of God that I encounter bring nothing but hurt into my life, it becomes very difficult to believe He is a good God who loves abundantly. The only times I've ever felt wanted was when I was with my friends. So I ask you, when I needed him the most, when I was hurting and broken and feeling worthless inside, where was your God?"

We had been walking for over two hours, and I expected him to refute everything I said, to get defensive or angry, *something*. Instead, he suggested we go for a cup of tea. As we sat down, my mind was reeling. Where was the anger and the violent shouting I was so used to? Yet in the gentlest voice he said: "I praise and thank God for giving me your company. I learned so much from you today."

I was speechless. Previous elders would never listen to me. Here was this man I hardly knew listening to me. We had spent two hours playing mental tug-of-war, with me aiming to pull the preacher into my atheistic mindset while remained rooted in his faith. In a single sentence, he

---

4   Bach, Richard (1978): *Illusions: The Adventures of a Reluctant Messiah.* London: Pan Books.

dismantled that idea. I realised in instant I was playing against nothing, pulling forcefully on rope with no strain and falling hard on the cold ground with this false, self-constructed illusion that I had won. And there was my opponent, standing calmly with an arm extended to uphold me. A smile on his face—not one of victory or superiority, but of compassion and understanding. I was shaken. We walked back to the camp in complete silence.

For the first time in years, I did not feel any pangs of negativity inside. The loneliness and depression that plagued me, even when I was teaching my beloved students, were damped down, and the inner darkness to which I had grown so accustomed had lightened. A completely unknown sense of peace around me. It was difficult to sleep that night. I replayed that meeting in my head over and over, trying to understand why it had such an impact on me.

*   *   *

The next morning, the congregation had a special event for the recovering alcoholics and drug addicts who lived in the other section—some of whom had only a short time to live. It was the last day of camp and everyone was ready to serve others. I was fluent in the local language so was asked to speak to them. The people in the hall were in very poor condition. Some of them had their cheeks, lip or chin surgically removed. It was a roomful of people who had reduced themselves to whispers of what they had once been, of what they could have been.

"Hello Sanjay!" A somewhat familiar voice broke my reverie. To my amazement, I recognised a junior from my school approach me.

"What are you doing out here?" I asked incredulously.

"You don't know? My parents kicked me out of the house…" He

tapered into silence.

"No… I didn't." My voice was barely above a whisper.

"I haven't been a very good boy." Sadness soaked his words. I didn't know what to say. "Sanjay, please take me out of here. Please!" His face was desperate, and he grabbed my arm with both his hands, getting progressively tighter and tighter. Tears streaming down his face, he cried "I can't stay here any longer. Please take me. Please!"

The praise and worship of my fellow camp mates began to ring throughout the hall, passionate, enthusiastic, and joyful as ever. I was confused and felt totally helpless. The juxtaposition of this pathetic man and the ecstatic sounds of worship was heartbreaking. I always thought that if one of my friends needed me, I would readily give anything to help them. But I didn't know what I could do for this man. His cries were getting louder, more desperate. His grip tightened.

"Please! I don't want to stay here anymore. I'm begging you!"

I wanted to relieve him of this pain and misery, but I didn't know how. Looking around at the sullen faces of the people, I started seeing the faces of my friends who were addicted to drugs and alcohol as the boy's words rang in my ears. "Please help me. Please help me. Please help me!" My heart exploded with an overwhelming sense of empathy and compassion, pouring out into streams of tears. I cried and cried for these people, hurting as if I was the one afflicted. Other members of the camp helped disentangle me and took me to a separate room. I continued to cry with worship in the background, the whole congregation ushering in the presence of God as I sobbed. I must have cried for more than an hour, drifting into a strange state of semi consciousness.

When I finally composed myself, I felt as if all my burdens had been lifted. I felt like I was a new person. I saw the world with new eyes, and it had never looked so beautiful. It was dramatic. Chains had been broken, and my body, my soul, my *spirit* felt free. I was filled with an unexplainable joy, and I couldn't wait to get home and tell my friends and family about it.

I was unable to take my friend away with me. I spoke to those who worked there and understood that this was the place where he gets the help and care he needed. His body was so damaged by the drugs, his mental and physical state deemed impossible for an unprepared person like me to help him on my own.

*   *   *

As soon as I arrived home I told my mother about all the miracles I experienced. She said she was happy I had a good time but dismissed any further significance of it.

The next day, I went to a friend who was renowned for his debating ability. I shared my camp experience with him, explaining how I felt like a new person.

"The Christians have brainwashed you," he said shortly. "Give it some time, and all this hype will wear off itself."

"Perhaps…," I replied.

I sat at home, deep in thought. Was it brainwashing? Did it actually happen? Maybe I had just been influenced by my surroundings, caught up in the moment. How was I going to verify the legitimacy of my experience? Then I remembered my school Bible. I fumbled in my study drawer. I held the book in my hands. I shut my eyes and said:

"Jesus, they say you are the true God." A pause as I searched for the right words. "If you are the true God, please answer me because I have no one else to look to. Did the Christians use the power of words to brainwash me?"

I gripped the Bible tightly, stopping for a moment before opening it randomly. My eyes fell on the page, and I read 1 Corinthians 2:1-5:

> *And so it was with me, brothers and sisters. When I came to you, I did not come with eloquence or human wisdom as I proclaimed to you the testimony about God. For I resolved to know nothing while I was with you except Jesus Christ and him crucified. I came to you in weakness with great fear and trembling. My message and my preaching were not with wise and persuasive words, but with a demonstration of the Spirit's power, so that your faith might not rest on human wisdom, but on God's power.*

I was awestruck. In my mind, the words kept flashing. *Not with wise and persuasive words, but with the demonstration of the spirit's power.* I knew in my heart that it had to be beyond natural human understanding. I was so desperate for an answer, and these verses made too much sense to me to be a coincidence.

The next day, I went back to my friend shared my experience.

"Whenever you ask for something, the universe will answer it," was his only response. According to him, there was no God, just a highly influential universe. "It was the Law of Attraction."

8

Blessed are the meek, for they shall inherit the world.

Mark 5:5

In spite of my friend's scepticism, I was on a new high, having just uncovered a whole new layer of life and meaning. I was still teaching martial arts sessions, which included children from both the slums and from wealthy families. I was touched by the respect, love, and dedication of these students and I found myself asking, who is actually poor?

The kids that society deemed poor and unworthy were some of the most loyal people I knew. They had so little, but they were ready to sacrifice much for me. They had big dreams and were not ready to give up on them, striving for a better life. They were so determined to make their loved ones proud and to ensure they were always protected. I was a role model to them, and they followed me attentively with complete focus. I was fascinated by their stories about everyday struggles and everything they needed to do to make ends meet at such a young age. It filled me with compassion that these deprived kids still knew how to love, laugh, and live. They did not have money but they were rich in heart. There was a sense of raw, unadulterated humanity about them, untainted by the world.

They were willing to connect with me so beautifully in a very real way when they threw me a surprise birthday party. The morning of my birthday, I went to our lesson as usual and noticed they were dressed in their best. I was then told to stand behind a tree until they called. A couple of the boys instructed me to keep my eyes closed as they guided me.

"Open!" they shouted.

I found myself in the middle of the field where we practiced. They were standing in two rows at attention holding a cake, marching towards me with military precision. They placed the cake before me and saluted. When I blew out the candles, we all burst into shouts of joy, excitement, and laughter. I was so touched and felt so loved and honoured, tears came to my eyes. I thanked them all for such a wonderful surprise.

"Sir, we didn't know how to honour you," they said. "So when we saw how the president was honoured on Republic day, we decided to follow suit."

I was so touched by this statement and wanted to return the same level of appreciation. I took them all to the only restaurant that was open at that time of the morning to enjoy a meal together. It was an unforgettable moment.

Those perfectly childlike and innocent interactions that made me wonder, who is actually poor?

*   *   *

I was preparing breakfast one Sunday, and searching the radio for music channel. I moved the dial and suddenly caught a voice saying, "Have you ever asked yourself this question: Who is poor?"

I almost froze. The speaker went on, "Generally speaking we assume anyone who does not have money is poor, or someone who cannot afford food, shelter or clothing is poor, but in this world everyone is poor. It could be poor in health, poor in character, poor in love, poor in discipline, poor in compassion, poor in joy, poor in knowledge, poor in understanding, poor in wisdom, poor in courage, poor in confidence, poor in spirit, poor in humility. Everybody in this world is poor and at the same time everyone in this world is rich, for no man is so poor that he is unable to give."

Then he quoted from the Bible, Matthew 5:3: *Blessed are the poor in spirit, for theirs is the kingdom of heaven.* He said that God resists the proud and gives grace to the humble, which is why we are commanded to love one another and help those in need. Meekness means strength under control, without pride.

I couldn't believe this coincidence. Here I was, suddenly getting a direct answer to the question I was currently searching. I was astonished to find that I had accidentally tuned into a radio channel from Hong Kong! The message on the radio touched something deep within my heart and encouraged me to keep giving, loving and forgiving.

That night, I was considering the chain of events after the Christian camp and how the universe was answering all my questions through the Bible and now the radio. I felt that perhaps somebody was out there, watching me, listening to and was giving me the answers for which I thirsted.

$$* \quad * \quad *$$

The lessons grew in popularity, and I increased the length from two to four hours. My concerned mother said:

"Son, I understand you enjoy your sports but I think you're spending too much time doing fruitless things. If you spent this amount of time doing productive work, you could be earning thousands!"

The truth was, I genuinely enjoyed teaching and giving. *We all have a moral obligation towards society. If you're not part of the problem, then you should be part of the solution.* Mr Wells's influence again, showing how deeply it was embedded in me. I connected with these children, and they warmed my heart everyday. Their continuous improvement motivated me to do more by them. Teaching, in my experience, is the best way to master any subject, and I felt like I was learning just as much as I was transmitting to them. I felt richer, more confident, more fulfilled.

But my mum had a point. Two hours was fine but four hours every morning was quite a lot. The Hindu teachings with which my family had raised me began to tap at my mental door. We were taught to obey our parents unconditionally, and I was afraid to turn my back on that. So when my mum expressed her feelings about my teaching, I began to think, Was I really wasting my time?

I started to calculate how much I could have been earning if all those hours were dedicated to "productivity." I reckoned it was about 30,000 rupees, a handsome amount at that time. It began to trouble me that I could have been earning a decent amount of money that could help my mother.

I met up with an accountant friend. During our catch-up, he mentioned that he was looking for newly constructed properties in which he could invest. Later that evening, I later bumped into another old acquaintance, a real estate dealer who happened to have such a property. I put them in touch with each other, and a deal was quickly made. I was entitled to a commission: 30,000 rupees. I felt this was a sign, as though God was looking after me. Maybe it wasn't brainwashing after all.

*   *   *

Feeling rather content and fulfilled in my newfound salvation, I started thinking, what *more* was I supposed to do with my life? What is my calling? It's funny how God chooses to speak to you. Sometimes He speaks in a moment of desperation as a boy seeks truth in an old Bible, sometimes through a radio. This time it was an advertisement for people who struggled with addiction. In bold letters, the caption said, "Just say NO."

Instantly the scene from the rehabilitation centre came flashing back into my mind. I was struck with an immediate sense of urgency, and I felt in my heart that now was the time to equip myself to help my friends drowning in drugs and alcohol. I approached Calcutta Samaritans and set out to tackle this problem. The Samaritans welcomed any voluntary help that was offered to them. I was accepted.

I was introduced to the counsellor in charge, a young, kind, soft-spoken lady who wanted to make sure I wasn't an addict myself. After going through my history and asking why I wanted to join the Samaritans, I was informed of the rules. For now, I could sit, observe, and listen. I would only be allowed to advise or comment when she was convinced I was ready to do so.

I was incredibly nervous sitting in on the first group and had no idea what to expect. The session started with the counsellor, Miss Kothari, gently asking one of the members how her weekend had been. I was not prepared for the amount of tears and pain that I was about to witness. This woman told of her abusive alcoholic husband who would come home every night, drunk and violent. She told the group how she would lock her two children in a room to protect them from being assaulted. It became all the more difficult when she revealed that he was "a very nice man when he was sober." To soothe her pain, she had been smoking marijuana and now couldn't cope without it. The physical, mental, emotional, and financial price was beginning to catch up to her.

This was a completely foreign world to me. There were people here from so many different walks of life, and I had no idea how to empathise with most of them. Each one was tortured with inner pain and heart-rending stories that had brought them to this point of desperation and I heard more and more stories, all the "why" questions of my life returned. My feelings of spiritual contentment began to falter.

One day, I was walking through the college chapel, thinking deeply about the resurrected questions. I glanced around the chapel and saw a familiar face smiling in recognition.

"Sir! It's nice to see you!" I greeted my old teacher, Mr Wells

"I'm surprised to see you here, Sanjay. How have you been? Oh, and don't call me 'sir' anymore for I have just been ordained a priest. Call me Father Wells."

"Sir…I will try but I think it will be difficult to change your title. How did you become a priest?" He seemed unfazed by the title, but he sighed as he recounted the story.

"My mother was in hospital with a heart problem. All the doctors had given up hope so I prayed to God to heal my mother. I said I would give my life for His service and become a priest if she was healed. I was desperate and ready to do anything for her. Well, as you can see, my mother recovered and I am fulfilling my promise."

I was in awe. His dedication to God and love for his mother were incredible. It was a whole new side to the severe, punishing man I knew many years ago. He smiled at me.

"I still follow every rule and principle you taught me, Sir," I started to say. The words came out in a rush. "No matter what the consequence might be. I just want to thank you. I am a happy misfit in society because of the impact you had in my life. I think I've become the man of principles and morals that you wanted us to be, and I hope I've made you proud." My heart fluttered nervously. I didn't know how he would take this. But I felt that I needed him to know the impact his lessons had on me.

He looked deeply into my eyes and said, "I am so sorry! It was wrong of me to treat you all the way I did in school. I have realised my mistake. I was studying in the Vatican, finding things on non-violence, peace, and tolerance and it's really opened my eyes to a bigger and better world."

I cracked. His apology brought back all the pain and hurt from my school days: the lashings, the broken friendships and the heartache that came from the people I loved when I chose to be honest with them. Tears rolled down my face.

"Sir, it's so hard to survive in society with all these principles and rules to follow!"

"Sanjay! If they crucified our God of Truth, what chance do we have? Remember truth always comes at a price."

He smiled and said goodbye. The whole incident dissolved as if it were a dream, those final words ringing in my ears. In the years to come, I would find out how true those words were as I thought more about power, desire, and treasure.

9

In a time of deceit, telling the truth is a revolutionary act.

George Orwell

On October 31, 1984 at approximately 9:15AM, Indian Prime Minister Indira Gandhi was walking through the gardens of her residence. At 9:20, she was assassinated by her two Sikh bodyguards, shaking the foundations of my country. This triggered a violent uproar in Delhi spreading to the edges of India. The ensuing chaos resulted in 2,700 deaths, with 20,000 people fleeing the city because of the riots. Sikh neighbourhoods became epicentres of violence in Delhi as innocent Sikhs were targeted.

We worried about our Sikh peers who were victimised by the widespread anger, revenge, and hate. As I watched news stories showing the death toll rise, the families that were broken, and the livelihoods lost. These people's fates were completely changed by those they once considered friends. It was sickening.

My group of friends pooled our resources to help the victims. But there was a profound sense of helplessness, as the world around us crumbled into a jungle of darkness. People became self-proclaimed judge, jury and executioner all in one, destroying lives in the name of religion. And why? God, why? How did humanity descend to the level that could easily destroy lives? Gang violence and mob fury was the norm, and I had discovered a world unlike the one I knew.

My disillusion extended beyond the news headlines. Success seemed to come only to the lying, cheating, and rich. Meekness was seen as weakness not strength, simplicity as stupidity, and humility was timidity. I questioned repeatedly what human power compels them to murder someone? What's going on in their minds to justify that behaviour? Is there any remorse or guilt? What is the greatest power, the greatest treasure a man can have?

For some time, I had been regularly visiting the British Library in Calcutta attempting to quench my thirst for knowledge. Now I had more direction as I scoured the shelves for an explanation to society's downward spiral I came across Vernon Coleman's *The Drugs Myth* where I found my answer.

> *...the cornerstones of our modern world are selfishness, greed, anger and hatred. Too few people talk, listen or help one another. The family unit has been shattered by progress. The driving forces we are taught to respect are greed and ambition.*
>
> *During the last fifty years or so, we have changed our world almost beyond recognition. Advertising agencies, television producers and newspaper editors have given us new aims to strive for, new hopes, new ambitions and new aspirations. At the same time, they have also given us*

new fears and anxieties. With the aid of psychologists and clever advertising, copywriters have learned to exploit our natural apprehensions. The advertisers have created ever expanding demands for new and increasingly expensive but worthless products. Our world has been turned upside down. Values and virtues have been turned inside out. Tradition, dignity and craftsmanship have been pushed aside in the constant search of profitability.

Society does not want to educate people. Society doesn't want people to broaden their horizon. Society wants obedience. Society knows that obedience will fit neatly into whatever hierarchy may exist and will put loyalty above honesty and integrity.

As we become materially richer and more powerful so we seem to become spiritually more deprived and individually more afraid. The more we acquire, the more we seem to need and the more we learn, the more we seem condemned by our ignorance. The more control we have of our environment, the more damage we do to it and to ourselves. The more successful we become in financial terms, the more we seem determined to destroy the qualities and virtues which lead to happiness and contentment. The more we learn about other worlds, the more we seem to forget our private duties and responsibilities to one another.

As manufacturers and advertisers have skillfully and deliberately translated our wants into needs, so we have exchanged generosity and caring for greed and self concern. Politicians, teachers, parents and scientists have encouraged each succeeding generation to convert simple dream and aspirations into fiery-no-holds-barred ambitions. In the name of progress, we have sacrificed common sense, goodwill and thoughtfulness and the gentle, the weak and the warm hearted have been trampled upon by hoards of embittered millions who have been taught to think only of the future and never the present or the past.[5]

Accuracy of his observations made so much sense to me. The passage of the text still resonates with me as I observe menaces in humanity. Why do people lie could so often in the name of *religion* was still a mystery to me.

I read a psychology article that explained that lying is just part of life, and that there are essentially two types of lying: concealing true statements or presenting false information as the truth. We lie for self-preservation, to escape, for gain, and to spare feelings. I realised I had been guilty, too. In school, students lied to escape punishment, to exaggerate, or to impress our friends. But these were tiny offences compared with those of people in power. The news was full of reports about religious leaders, businessmen, and politicians embezzling, taking bribes, and conning innocent people. But it was ordinary people who bore the brunt of the condemnation of dishonesty by these same leaders. I wasn't ok with these double standards So who was really corrupt?

Corruption was everywhere, so common that people accepted it as the norm. I was reminded that for most people it was all about survival. Even the noblest professionals were subjected to corruption, focusing on money instead of their role in society. "Honesty is the best policy" was long forgotten and replaced with "If you want something done, bring money because everyone has a price."

I had learned about the world's function, and yet I was still naive. When I was applying for a passport, the officer came to my home to verify my identity and to interview me. My mother had food ready for him as he interrogated me. Eventually, he steered the conversation and spoke of his tough life and how much he appreciated generous people who took care of him and his family, obviously dropping hints.

---

5   Coleman, Vernon (1992): *The Drugs Myth: Why the Drug Wars Must Stop*. Green Print.

"Doesn't the government pay you enough so that you don't need to depend on others?" The words escaped my mouth before I could catch them. He turned to my mother, his face burned red with anger.

"Your son doesn't know about the reality of the world. He's going to find himself in big trouble soon if he's not careful," he said pointedly.

"I'm so sorry for him," my mother apologised. "He's just a simple person and doesn't know much about the world yet."

"Young man," the officer spoke. "I am letting you go because of your mother. Otherwise I would have blacklisted you, and you would never get your passport."

Mum's look of desperation told me to stay quiet. She prepared plenty of gifts and sweets for him and his family. I will never forget the sarcastic smile he gave me as he left. That night, I couldn't sleep and wanted to do *something*. I couldn't stand the corruption anymore and resolved to apply for the special police force to fight the corruption.

I joined the voluntary sector of the local police force as a special officer. It was a fantastic chance to help people from a position of power. I clung to the principles imbued in me by my mother and my earliest teachers. My ability to make friends stood me in good stead as an officer, I was respected. I confess that I enjoyed the warmth of popularity as well as the feeling of making a difference in people's lives.

*   *   *

The Telegraph Calcutta, was holding an annual debate on the topic: Is Corruption a Way of Life? There were prominent speakers from all over the country, representing both sides of the argument. The debate attracted the huge audience. People were waiting eagerly for the intellectual drama that was surely about to take place. As expected, the speakers were incredibly eloquent and intelligent. A humble looking lady, took to the stage. From her first words, the audience was hooked.

She told a story of a king who threatened that anyone caught stealing should be hanged to death. Three people were caught stealing cattle and were arrested. They were brought in front of the king and asked if they had any final requests. Two of them asked for their favourite food. The third one said, "Your Majesty, I have been a thief all my life and never been caught. I have some grains of rice made of gold in my house that I stole years ago. My last wish is to sow those grains in the soil, water them and watch a shoot blossom." There was uproar among the court. Grains of gold blossoming into shoots? The thief is clearly mad! Nevertheless, the king ordered his soldiers to search for the grains. The soldiers returned, golden rice in hand and everyone was in disbelieving awe. The thief planted the grains while everyone watched. Nothing happened.

"Your Majesty, I forgot to mention, the grains will only grow when someone who has never stolen in his life pours the water. Why don't you pour the water?" The king was taken aback.

"I can't… When I was a child, I used to steal sweets from the kitchen."

"General, sir, what about you?"

"I can't," the general stammered, looking embarrassed. "To become rich and powerful, I stole land from my family." The thief turned to the priest.

"Your grace, why don't you pour the water?"

"I can't," said the priest, face flushed. "My lust for success was so great, I stole books to become knowledgeable."

The king, who was watching and getting progressively more frustrated raised his voice.

"Prisoner! Is there any point to your madness?"

"Your Majesty! The point I am trying to make is that everybody here, including yourself, has admitted to stealing but I am the one being hanged because I was caught. You are all thieves but get away with it because you are not caught."

The speaker concluded her speech, saying, "Is corruption a way of life? Yes. We are all corrupt in some form or another but we get away with it because we are not caught."

The audience was astonished and gave her a standing ovation. It was an eye-opener for us all. We all have our moments of weakness, our own short comings and blind spots. It was the blunt truth of life. We are all guilty of wrongdoings and are capable of corruption. Therefore we must all work towards honesty it or risk hypocrisy.

*   *   *

Considering my childhood, it's hardly surprising that I was especially suspicious of religious leaders. Their actions rarely matched their words, and I found myself wondering about their secret to success. I could understand why greedy businessmen would bow to dishonesty to advance their wealth, but not the people responsible for the moral standard. My mistrust and anger towards them grew.

Following orders was difficult for me because I was restless, impatient and highly strung. I had years of emotional and mental abuse scarring me. I hated being looked down on, disrespected, and ordered around. Of course, the exceptions were my mother and teachers. Anyone else I would stand up to when they were being harsh and cruel for no reason. It was as if there were two sides to me. My heart was sensitive and fearful, craving warmth and gentleness. And my mind, after enduring years of torture, had developed a reactionary defense mechanism. When my heart was hurt, my mind took over, protecting me from aggression.

I would stand up for the weak and fight for the underdog. I was fiercely independent. Even if food was sent to me by a neighbour, I wouldn't eat it. I never asked for favours, and if someone helped me I would feel indebted to them and repay kindness.

I was at a friend's party and was introduced to his cousin who had just finished his course at the Institute of Hotel Management and was planning to start his own catering and events business. We immediately clicked, and he soon proposed we become partners. I was excited. He had a place with one of the city's most powerful hoteliers and he was my connection. It seemed an unbelievable stroke of luck.

The hotel planned to open a fast food outlet to compete with the mainstream franchises. We had a month to refurbish their location. I was nervous but excited to see the project take off. Together my business partner and I worked for 26 days nonstop to get the place up and running. Aside from a few minor hitches, everything came together, and it was ready to serve burgers, pizza, and ice creams by the deadline.

We were quick to attract a diverse crowd. It was the first time in a while that I was able to forget about all the bitterness I felt towards society. I was enjoying the warmth and popularity. We had media coverage, arranged saleswomen attracted a large male following. But; if anyone disrespected or misbehaved around any of the girls, they were kicked out.

We were open late, so our place became a meeting point for the staff from the area restaurants. We were exchanging our experiences. Powerful businessmen started to join. They would pick us up after closing take us to various hotels as their party guests. Being fluent in English added to their sophisticated reputation as many of them couldn't speak it. They would drink long into the night and were thoroughly shocked when I declined to imbibe every single night.

Most of them were in the restaurant business they inherited from their parents at a young age which meant no time for further education. Their dreams, their struggles, their exploits and victories were all so inspiring to me that I hung onto every word as they chatted. But my inclusion on these nights out also meant watching women dancing to Bollywood music. The blatant objectification of them made me deeply uncomfortable. I discouraged the behaviour and, after much persistence, convinced them to check out some classier clubs instead.

We partied every night. Everywhere we went, people admired and respected our group. It was a heady feeling and it increased the business. Soon, we were able to introduce the wedding catering and big parties. The success of the business and the honest money earned was worth the hard work. I hadn't cheated or lied to anyone, and my business partner and I led our team well. Things were going great.

I loved to dance. The music flowed through my body and I was free. I didn't know fatigue or frustration until the music stopped. And then pangs of loneliness would creep in again. Dancing was my drug with which I tried to fill an internal emptiness. I knew how to play my part for an audience, when to smile, when to laugh. But it was a mask covering a feeling of meaninglessness. My church camp experience and burgeoning faith became distant memories.

One evening my business partner was talking to two shady-looking men outside the club. He told me not to speak to them as he was in charge. I was confused and watched him entertain them with food and drinks before saying goodbye. I asked what was going on.

"Those guys represent the local mafia," he told me "We've been doing so well lately, and it got their attention. They were collecting protection money." I was speechless at first. This wasn't anything like the glamour of *The Godfather* I had loved so much. This was real.

"It's okay," he continued. "My friend knows someone even more powerful than these guys. We'll visit him tomorrow."

My understanding of the world shifted again. The next day, we headed to a restaurant owned by a local don. His outfit was a bunch of bookmakers who owned race horses, real estate, bars, and restaurants. The place was huge, filled with dimly lit tables, some surrounded for privacy. We were greeted warmly and led to a curtained table. Refreshments were served. My business partner leaned closer to me and quickly whispered, "Please, Sanjay, just for today forget about your principles and just drink with these guys. I don't want to displease them."

My stomach squirmed, I didn't want to endanger the business or our lives. There was no way I would drink. When the drinks were being served, I politely refused.

"Sorry..." I began, "I don't drink on principle. If I've offended anyone, I am ready to leave."

My partner was glaring at me, sweat forming on his forehead, fear obviously in his eyes. The don and his men looked at me for a moment, and my heart skipped a beat.

"Brother, we see a lot of people from different backgrounds every day," the don said. "As such, we are a great judge of character, and I can honestly say you are certainly unique. I respect your principles. People like you are hard to find."

In a single moment, all tension was released. Even in this unfamiliar underworld, character and principles were valued. I was vindicated. The don was questioning my background and confided in me that the only reason he was in this business was because he inherited it. He wanted more honorable life for his children.

"I would love it if my kids turned out like you. A man of character, sticking to his principles". He invited me to be a private tutor to his children and their cousins.

I agreed, stunned at the honour as well as at his high regard for my character. He also refused to smoke or drink and set high standards for his children to follow.

As we left he said, "You're both good guys. You're leaders full of integrity that you don't see these days. Leave it to me, no one will bother you for protection money or anything else. I'll make sure of that."

From that day on, we knew we were safe. I started tutoring his kids and loved being in their lives. They studied at a posh boarding school and had very good manners. I became very close to their family, and it gave me a glimpse of a usually hidden world.

*   *   *

Our business was thriving. We had so many customers from different backgrounds. Our location was great, in the middle of the city in one of the richest streets in town. With such diversity, we were often invited to different religious groups. I was at my Christian friend's house and had just crossed the threshold into his home when a Sikh-turned-Jehovah's Witness introduced himself to me and we started chatting.

"Do you think there is evil in this world?" he asked.

"Of course there is. Lots of it," I replied with no hesitation. I could see he was taken aback by the promptness of my reply.

I continued, "The world is full of liars, manipulators, and cheaters. Basically every religious sect is led by them, and our politicians who are supposed to be on our side lie to us all the time. The world is full of hypocrites and con artists."

Looking flustered, he opened a magazine and showed me a beautiful picture of earth and heaven.

"If you follow Jehovah," he began, "you will be able to live in heaven. Only 144,000 people can go to heaven."

"I didn't know God had booking agents out here," I joked, incredulous. The concept just seemed bizarre to me. As we continued to speak, I noticed that he wasn't actually listening to what I had to say. He was just blurting out well-rehearsed statements. But I'm not the type to back down, so I argued back passionately. My interest in public speaking and psychology definitely gave me an edge in this conversation. I knew that good salesmen do their research, anticipating questions so they can be armed with the answer. That's exactly what he was doing, and I did my best to throw him off track.

It felt like a really intense tennis match. Every time he attacked me with a question, I pounced back immediately. It was exhilarating. It was like I was dancing again. That same level of release and freedom, the control and joy, it was all there in that moment of intellectual competition. Again I felt my insecurities fade into the background.

"Look," his tactic changed. "I am here to share with you an important message. Let me show you a Bible scripture from Revelations 21:3-4. 'With that I heard a loud voice from the throne say: "Look! The tent of God is with mankind, and He will reside with them, and they will be His people. And God Himself will be with them. And He will wipe out every tear from their eyes, and death will be no more, neither will mourning nor outcry nor pain be anymore. The former things have passed away."' What do you think about that? Does it sound good to you?"

He looked at me, a kind of triumph in his eyes. He was trying to get me into a corner, forcing me to answer more questions and give my opinions. I had seen my grandfather use this technique time and time again. Whenever he quoted Hindu scriptures to impress people, he showed his intellectual dominance. They were forced to give opinions on things taken out of context that they didn't fully understand. They often ended up looking quite foolish, and he got his way.

I had too much experience with false humility and fancy words. I knew too many gurus and "men of God" who only wanted to con people in God's name. I could tell the difference between genuinely honest people and those with sharp tongues talking about love and salvation. After some time, the Jehovah's Witness realised I wasn't easy to crack.

"I'm an atheist," I told him frankly. "I don't believe any of the arguments you're presenting. I'll visit your kingdom hall, though, and show you that nothing is going to change."

So, their next meeting, I went to meet their leader. The building was huge, neat, and very well-organised. It was a very neutral-feeling place, reminiscent of my school assembly hall. As I entered, I was impressed by how well-dressed the congregation was as they chatted or welcomed new people. I was met by a very warm greeting and directed to my seat as the meeting began. It opened with a song and a prayer followed by 30 minutes of an elder's sermon. The elder spoke about Adam and how he gave each animal in the world their name. Another hymn followed, concluding with what was called a "Watchtower Study." In the study, an article was read paragraph by paragraph, and members of the audience raised their hands to respond to questions from the study, but no one asked any questions of their own.

This is more like a public speaking training school, I thought to myself. Designed to brainwash people and teach them to brainwash other people. The lack of questions from the members was unnerving. During the sermon, the elder kept putting down traditional churches, saying that they asked for offerings and conned people into believing Christ was born on Christmas Day. He told the members to shut their ears to what people say to them when they're evangelizing—in other words to talk *at* people instead of *with* them. It was a very "us versus them" mentality, and it made me incredibly uncomfortable.

At the end of the service, all of this "training" was put into practise as they threw all their well-rehearsed lines at me. I told them bluntly that I didn't believe that converting to their group was the way to get to heaven.

"People only join you guys because they're afraid of death. And because they want to be someone and feel safe in a group." I said, boldly. I could tell that people were getting upset that I wasn't backing down.

"I'll come prepared next time," I concluded, before leaving.

*   *   *

Not long after, a friend of mine introduced me to his brother-in-law who had been born into a Jehovah's Witness family and indoctrinated from a young age. He told me that as he grew up, there was a long list of rules he had to follow. He couldn't receive or give Christmas and birthday gifts, stand and salute the national flag, or even sing the national anthem. He wasn't allowed to do any sports or join any school clubs. He was discouraged from participating in school plays and later from attending college, although how much of that was to do specifically with his religion I'm not sure. And, although he wanted to become a police officer or join the military, his parents were so controlling that he redirected his dreams elsewhere. Christian literature and music were taboo, as were more traditional churches and crucifix symbols. Blood transfusions and donations were also prohibited. Mother's and Father's Day were not celebrated. Even his friends were monitored heavily by his parents and his inner circle had to be made up of Jehovah's Witnesses. Even saying "bless you" when someone sneezed wasn't allowed!

It blew my mind how controlling his family had been. It sparked a curiosity in me about other spiritual groups that I interacted with frequently, especially Christian sects. I didn't understand the Bible properly at this stage and was still trying to understand the concept of love, sin, creation, heaven, hell, God, salvation and the Holy Trinity. It was a lot. The more I listened to each sect, the more confused I became. I visited many organisations, researching each one and finding the experts in their field. Each sect had some kind of demand for submission and exclusivity, a persecution complex, control and isolation of its members, all in the pursuit of salvation.

I was always confused by the last part. Who exactly was this savior, Jesus? Each sect gave a very animated explanation of who Jesus was to them, and with each conflicting answer, my brain became more and more muddled. Jehovah's Witnesses' Jesus is actually the archangel, Michael. He is God's first creation and Satan's brother. To Hindus, Jesus was a guru, an *acharya* (one who teaches by example) that confirms everyone can realise their own "God-consciousness" as Christ proclaimed he and the father are one. He was equated to the Lord Krishna who essentially preached the same message. This view perpetuated the idea that everyone was the same being, and rather than loving your neighbour, we should act in unity like we were intended to.

A Muslim friend revealed to me that yes, they believed Jesus was born of a virgin and that he was also the miracle-working messiah that Christians know and would return in the last days to establish world peace. Christian Science argues that Jesus was human and Christ was the divine idea. The most shocking explanation was from The Children of God who believed that angel Gabriel lay with Mary to conceive Jesus and that Jesus had sexual relations with Martha and Mary.

Atheists and other secular groups links details from the story of Jesus to earlier mythologies, including the virgin birth, prophecies, constellations on the night of his birth, the wise men, infant persecution, miracles, and the crucifixion story. These details are found in the story of Egyptian god

Horus, Greek Attis and Dionysus, Indian Krishna, and Persian Mithras. After discovering all this, I was more lost than ever before. Who was Jesus?

But even without untangling the mystery of Jesus, after all the research I had conducted, I felt more than sufficiently equipped to fight back against anyone preaching from the Christian faith. My negative experience with religion and religious leaders made me want to take down anything associated with God. I felt like I had all the answers. I started visiting Christian groups for the sole purpose of refuting their beliefs. On one of my visits, a member told me they had nicknamed me the Devil's Advocate. I wasn't offended at all. I was actually quite proud that I was getting to them.

One day, a Christian friend invited me to an apologetics seminar that defended the Christian faith. He mentioned that only 300 people were chosen from the country and I was one of them. My ego liked that. I immediately agreed to come. I was looking forward to asking them difficult questions and putting them to shame. But as it says in Proverbs 16:18, "Pride goes before destruction, a haughty spirit before a fall." I was not even slightly prepared for what was to come.

*   *   *

Ravi Zacharias grew up in an Anglican household but was an atheist until the age of 17 when he tried to commit suicide. While he was in hospital, a Christian worker brought him a Bible and told his mother to read from John 14.

"Because I live, you will also live," his mother's voice gently read verse 19, and something resounded in young Ravi's heart. This was his only hope. A new way of living—life defined by the ultimate Author. In that moment, he committed his life to Christ, promising that he would leave no stone unturned in his pursuit of Truth. In 1966, Ravi moved to Canada with his family and graduated from Bible College in 1972.

And now, I was watching him speak at a conference. I wasn't sure what to expect. As the panel began, it was completely different from what I was expecting. The theme was the existence of God, and I found many of the points rather striking. He asked the crowd, "If there was no God, where did everything come from? Why is there intelligent life and does it have any meaning?" They questioned the human conscience, arguing that understanding good and evil had to come from somewhere higher than ourselves. Because without it, morality is relative, and we wouldn't have a unified idea of what really is evil. But here we are, everyone agreeing that lying and murder are inherently wrong. That can't simply be human opinion. No, something larger was at work there.

Ravi went on to argue that in a Godless world, there is no hope. Suffering serves no purpose if there is no eternal life where reparations are made. And while people might find comfort in thinking there is no God to blame, that also means there is no God to give us strength, meaning, or comfort. In this light, there was only madness and confusion in the wake of suffering and evil.

Finally, if there was no God, our existence simply does not make sense. How can we explain our desires and search for purpose and fulfilment without Him? Humanity naturally searches for something spiritual and meaningful. It has to have come from somewhere.

The way Ravi argued his points was new to me. I was used to people spouting off doctrine without really arguing their point properly. But he was impressive. He knew so much on so many subjects and was humble about it when he didn't know the answer to my questions.

"If the Bible says to love your enemies, and Satan is God's enemy, does that mean we should love Satan?" I asked during question time.

"You can love him, but that doesn't mean you have to obey him," he said simply. It was brilliant. I asked question after question and was astonished by his answers. For the first time in my life, I realised that the people who actually knew their Bible weren't ignorant or shallow. In contrast to them, I knew nothing. I knew I had to start again.

After lunch that day, I was surprised to find Ravi Zacharias approach me and sit at my table. I was nervous but gathered all my courage to ask him, "What is the purpose of all these things we talk about here?"

He put his arm around me gently, smiled warmly and spoke in a kind voice. "Son, the whole purpose of this conference is to make people think. Everyone—pantheists, atheists, skeptics, polytheists—has to answer these questions. What is life's meaning? What happens to me when I die? Those are fulcrum points of our existence." I was surprised by his answer. It sounded so simple but so profound. I admired his humility, intelligence, warmth, and humour.

The next day of the conference, there were workshops that we could choose from. I chose the one on cults. The person leading asked if any of us had any experience with cults. I raised my hand and explained a little about my religious upbringing and my attendance at religious services that I found problematic. He invited me to speak and conduct the workshop for a bit. I found that I thoroughly enjoyed facilitating. I loved answering questions and guiding the discussion. I realized, too, that there was still so much for me to learn. This had been an overwhelmingly positive experience, which I was not expecting. I knew it was time to study some more. I returned home with a different perspective and a bit more humility.

*   *   *

Back home, I continued on my quest for knowledge, but I was

working and partying hard, too. But even back in the party culture, I changed my approach to people. Instead of standing aloof and turning a blind eye, I started confronting friends who were heavy drinkers or drug addicts, challenging them to sober up. But I gave them my word that I would be there for them every step of the way to recovery. They were shocked and defensive at first, giving me excuses to validate what they were doing. But I was persistent, and, eventually many of my friends opened up and joined a recovery programme. It warmed my heart to see them get the help they needed. In those moments, Mr Wells's voice would echo in my mind again. *We all have a moral obligation towards society; if you are not part of the problem, you should be part of the solution.*

It was during this time that I heavily researched the 12-step programme to understand the nature of addiction and the recovery process. The deeper I went, the more I realised my own life was undergoing just as much change the friends actually going through the recovery process.

Part Four

Chronicles

10

God grant me the serenity to accept
the things I cannot change;
courage to change the things I can;
and wisdom to know the difference.
Serenity Prayer, Reinhold Niebuhr

As I continued to research, I discovered that addiction was much more complicated than I first thought. It wasn't just the physical act of repeated substance abuse. There were multiple facets to it. Addiction as a whole was the repeated and compulsive seeking and use of a substance that has negative effects on the person. It's a disease that keeps taking away.

Eventually, addicts move on as their tolerance for a certain substance naturally increases, and so they sometimes requires more alcohol or drugs to get the same effect. In extreme cases, people develop a physical dependence on a substance, where they exhibit signs of withdrawal when they don't get their fix. It happens when there are physical changes in the brain. At this point, it is no longer a matter of willpower, but of physiology.

The stories I heard from recovering addicts deeply touched my heart. I attended many Alcoholics Anonymous meetings just to keep learning about the whole process. When it came to alcoholism, I found that despair poisoned their hope and, their world was void of joy. They were alone and trapped, slaves to alcohol, handing control over to the bottle. Their peace of mind, body and spirit were destroyed. Many alcoholics didn't think breaking the cycle was possible after many failed attempts. Yet here they were.

Although the 12-step programme has Christian roots, the only requirement for AA membership is a desire to stop drinking. They're based on the experiences of programme founders, who now aim to help other addicts. These 12 steps are:

1) Admit powerlessness over alcohol and their lives have become unmanageable

2) Believe that a Power greater than themselves can restore them to sanity

3) Make a decision to turn their will and lives over to the care of God as they understood Him

4) Make a searching and fearless moral inventory of themselves

5) Admit to God, to themselves and to another human being the exact nature of their wrongs

6) Be entirely ready to have God remove all defects of character

7) Humbly ask Him to remove their shortcomings

8) List all the people they had harmed and be willing to make amends with all of them

9) Make direct amends to said people when possible, except when to do so would injure them or others

10) Continue to take personal inventory and, when they were wrong,

promptly admit it.

11) Sought, through prayer and meditation, to improve their conscious contact with God as they understand Him, praying only for knowledge of His will and the power to carry that out

12) Having had spiritual awakening as a result of these steps, try to carry this message to alcoholics and practice these principles in all their affairs.

When I first attended a meeting, I was amazed by the honesty of the speakers. The first speaker I met was a man I will call Joseph.

"Dear friends," he began. "My name is Joseph and I'm an alcoholic. By the grace of God and this wonderful fellowship, I haven't had my first drink today."

As the session went on, I saw each step unfold in the lives of the people who spoke, all of whom were at different stages. Some speakers confessed the destructive nature of their lives. They admitted that they couldn't stop it on their own and acknowledged it had only gotten worse as they tried. So, they took the first step towards freedom by finding help and admitting just how bad their addiction was.

I was impressed to find the action steps that were always at the ready. Whether it was encouragement to abstain or letting go of pride, there was always a solution. If the person lacked power to control his drinking, the solution was to find an external source of power to remedy the problem and they'd be given the steps needed to tap into it. Each session would then end with the Serenity Prayer.

During this time of research, I became overly aware that life is continual battle. With circumstances, with everyday difficulties, with things that are important to us. To be happy, we need to know we belong, that we are wanted and valued. We have to know for ourselves that we are worth something—not because of what we can do, but for who we are. We need a sense of progress and achievement, to be successful. I read an interesting article that helped me understand this more deeply.

Abraham Maslow's hierarchy of needs[6] proposed that all humans have needs on five different levels. On the base level are our fundamental biological needs—things like food, drink, shelter. This is followed by safety needs (protection from elements, security and stability); belonging and love; esteem (achievements, self-esteem etc); and, finally, self actualisation. The final need is about realising personal potential and fulfilment. The hierarchy models how all people need to address each level, starting from the first and progressing to the latter stages. It's a process of development over the course of an individual's life and, without the lower order needs, the higher needs cannot be met.

After learning this, I came to realise that to understand someone's behaviour, we must first uncover what need they are trying to fulfil. Only when we can properly answer this question can we completely understand someone and help them make necessary changes. This knowledge became invaluable to me. Over the next season of my life, I continued working with my friend and volunteering with the Samaritans. I encouraged and inspired quite a number of people. And, to be honest, my life was changing too. I was happier and felt better helping the people around me. Maybe being able to help others was one of my lower needs, one of my great desires. It certainly felt like it was more than just an achievement—it was becoming a cornerstone of my life.

*   *   *

---

[6]   Maslow, A. H. (1943). A theory of human motivation. *Psychological Review, 50* (4), 370-396.

And yet, even in the midst of all this feeling of fulfilments and the good I was doing, there was still an emptiness nibbling on my insides. I was still partying, but no amount of business success, friends, or nights out had managed to fill that void. But I was very good at pretending otherwise.

The supernatural testimonies of the recovering addicts connecting with their higher power were incredible. After years, people would be healed of their addiction with prayer as their weapon. It made me wonder if prayer was a more powerful healer than medicine. Most of the people who shared their testimony were Christian, talking about the Holy Spirit and how the healing power of the name of Jesus transformed their life. I decided to visit the Assemblies of God Church in Calcutta to try to understand more about Jesus and the power of Christian prayer.

*   *   *

I stepped into an air conditioned building, long and circular sofas arranged neatly around the room. It was the first time I had seen such a large church. The Assemblies of God was known for doing great things for the underprivileged community in the city. The speaker that day speaker was a guest from America. He was warm, passionate, and funny. As a student of public speaking, I was impressed with the sermon. He talked about God's promises, quoting appropriate scriptures. Then he spoke about his own life, concluding that "God has kept all His promises in my life."

At the end of the service, I approached him and asked how he knew all the promises were true.

"I am living proof that all of God's promises have come true in my life." He replied humbly before excusing himself and departing. It was a simple answer and a simple service, but I walked away feeling good. The church environment was big but friendly. I also loved that the speaker was available to talk to. He was human and approachable, even though he was a religious leader. That was new but refreshing for me.

In my experience, preachers and leaders ignored you if you confronted them or asked a question in public. The reply I was used to hearing was, "You haven't reached my level yet." I hated it because it made me feel insignificant. My grandfather always used that excuse on me when I challenged any of his beliefs. But this speaker was different. He gave answers and listened to what others had to say.

When I told my friends about my experience the next day, I was immediately mocked. They bombarded me with a whole bunch of Christian, political, and secret society conspiracy theories. They tried to convince me that missionaries were actually CIA aiming to destroy the Indian culture for the benefit of America. It started getting out of hand so I suggested we talk about it in depth, properly, over dinner.

Soon after, we sat down to dinner to discuss the reality of conspiracy theories. We discussed British Imperialism and how the first British company snuck into India under the guise of traders and colonised our nation for the great agricultural and manufacturing benefits. It was about the gold. My friends went on to talk about how the British Empire had tainted Indian culture, created false religions and prophets, all for the sake of advancement and control. Hindus that lived peacefully with Muslims were suddenly pitted against them, presumably when leaders released falsities to incite anger between the two religious groups. What I was gathering was that British East India had poisoned the country and had ripped the social, religious, and cultural fabric so delicately stitched together. One friend believed this control was still being forced on India by major financial institutions like the Bank of England and the US Federal Reserve.

Another friend claimed that Jesus had actually travelled through

India, learning from gurus and that He used this knowledge in Israel to perform His miracles. He believed Krishna and Christ were the same person. Basically, my friends were trying to convince me there was an ongoing Christian conspiracy from the western world to enslave our nation. Churches, they pointed out, were exempt from tax and could say whatever they wanted, making it easy for secret agencies to carry out their business.

As crazy as it sounds now, they presented their case logically, using statistics and real data to back up their claims. I didn't know enough to refute their arguments, so, once again, it was time to study and research.

11

For the love of money is the root of all kinds of evil.
1 Timothy 6:11

Although I was still battling my inner demons, life was exciting. I had built up a trustworthy and respectful reputation for myself, gaining popularity because of my networking ability. People were asking me for favours or inviting me to high-end events in the city. I genuinely love people, so while these perks were fun, I didn't have an ulterior motive when helping them out. Eventually I became an event organiser, the most popular type of event being open-air rock shows. These events added to my fame, and I became a highly sought after and well connected person in the city. I was flooded with offers from the hospitality industries. They were very good positions, but I declined, much happier being my own boss.

At one point, I was approached by a religious leader who wanted my help to build a dark church, a congregation for the anti-Christ. When I met

Sanjay Gupta

with him, I instantly disliked him. He was shrewd and tried to use money as a motivator, tempting me with the connections he had all over the world, saying that I would not have such an opportunity ever again. I hated being spoken to like that, almost as if he was threatening me or wanted to control my decisions. Deep down, I burned with rage. Clearly, this man has no idea who I am, I thought. I am no ordinary person that can be lured with money, fame, or power. It felt like he was negotiating a price for my soul, for everything I stood for, and I wasn't going to let that happen. I valued integrity above all else, and no one could buy me out, especially in the name of religion.

"My soul is not for sale." I cut him off abruptly. The man was shocked. "I am not the kind of person you can mess around with," I continued. "I don't want to be part of whatever you're offering." He turned red with humiliation but his body language remained cold. I bid him goodbye, but really meant good riddance, and thought that was the end of it.

But for nights after the meeting, I was plagued with nightmares. It felt as if someone was trying to strangle or lift me in the air and drop me on the earth. It went on for weeks until one night, I woke up to go to the bathroom. Since my building was old and antiquated, the bathroom was located outside the house. It was pitch black, and as I made my way to the bathroom, I saw a figure creeping on the wall. It was a black snake. I froze in terror, not making a single sound or daring to move an inch and waited until it was gone. I lived in the heart of the city. Snakes climbing the side of a building were unheard of. I was spooked.

Another night, another strange and scary thing happened. I was once again on my way to the bathroom when I saw a white figure in the distance. At first, I thought it was someone from the building but as I approached him, I saw him bang his feet on the ground. Suddenly, my body was lifted

92

into the air and I lost consciousness.

When I opened my eyes, my mother was crying over me, and I was surrounded by people from the building. I asked her what happened and she could not speak, still crying. After some time, I realised I couldn't open my right eye. My body felt heavy and groggy, but I fought against it to look into the mirror. To my horror, my face was swollen like a balloon. My father was applying ice on my eyebrows, which were cut and bleeding.

I later discovered that the people in the building heard a loud bang. Upon investigation, they found my body. As if someone had lifted me up and banged my head on the stone wall. Luckily, I was okay.

"Your son is very fortunate," the doctor said the next day. "If the impact was even a millimetre lower, he would have cracked his skull and could have lost his right eye." The dent that is still in my right eyebrow is a scar I will forever hold. These weird and uncanny incidents kept haunting me for some time, chasing me in my mind. I needed time out so I went with a friend to the outskirts of the city to spend time with his cousin who lived with seven engineering graduates.

One Friday night, we got home late after watching the chariot festival. I was sharing a room with two other people, happy for the escape and company. After an eventful and fun night, we went to bed, and I felt peaceful. But the peace was short lived. I woke up in the middle of the night, feeling like someone was holding my left foot. I sprang out of bed as fast as I could, thinking one of the other guys was pranking me. I turned on the light but found both guys were fast asleep. Surely, they were both in on it and were feigning sleep. I woke them up and warned them that if they did it again, there would be consequences. In their foggy stupor, they protested sincerely. It wasn't them, they said, and for the time being, I was willing to leave it be.

I lay down for the second time that night, but as my head hit my pillow, I could hear strange noises. It was as if someone was digging, like iron rods piercing brick again and again. I thought my mind was playing games on me. I didn't even want to tell the guys what was happening, thinking they would call me a coward. I tried to ignore it and go back to sleep but the noise persisted.

Then the grabbing sensation returned, and I kicked in retaliation. My foot hit thin air but, on the way down, struck my friend sleeping on the floor near me. He woke up demanding an explanation. I turned on the light again, silently hoping that there was an intruder that could explain all this. When I saw nothing, I went to the kitchen and picked up a knife and candle and searched each room.

My search came up empty. Everyone in the flat was asleep and, rather than finding a prankster or intruder, I was met with sleepy protests and told not to worry about any of it. The lights stayed on for the night, just in case someone tried something again. The kitchen knife and slippers were at the ready for attack. My eyes began to fall shut, and I could hear the clock ringing in the distance. *Ding ding ding.* I was dozing off but in my half sleep, I saw both lights in the room switch off. As I reached out to turn them on, they flicked back on before I had even reached the switch.

A sudden crack of thunder cut through the night. Wind whipped the side of the building with great fervour. Dogs along the street were barking, adding to the chaotic fray. I was properly scared. I had no idea what was happening. After a couple of hours, it stopped. It was 4.30AM, and I finally fell into an exhausted sleep.

Later that morning, at the breakfast table, the others revealed that the house was a magnet for strange incidents. They told me that years ago, the owner of the house and his wife were trying to start a family. Their maid fell in love with him. Naturally, he rejected her, and, heartbroken, she jumped into a well and committed suicide. As the legend goes, her spirit haunts the house. There was also a rickshaw puller who used to get drunk every night beside the nearby pond. One night, in his drunken stupor, he slipped and drowned in the pond. Apparently, his spirit haunted the house too.

I didn't believe in ghost stories, nor did I want to start. But I couldn't deny the possibility of a spiritual or supernatural realm. I mean, I had experienced it before. When I was younger and worshipping the goddess Kali, I would feel a dark spirit in me, something that yearned for blood and sacrifice. I had seen people being possessed, speaking in strange voices, and demanding favours for their appeasement.

I pondered on all this for a moment. If there was so much dark power in the world, surely there must be light to balance it out. Hinduism had the lord Hanuman prayer to ward off troubles or spiritual attack. I never fully believed in it, but I knew a few verses from films and songs. But I needed more. I had to know what power would be above all powers.

*   *   *

When I returned home, I told the don about the eventful weeks that had just passed. He was amused and suggested I buy a new house for my mother. I didn't understand.

"We have been thinking about it for a while. We would like to make you an offer." He paused, watching for my reaction. I was definitely intrigued. He reminded me of the Godfather in that moment, and I trusted him.

"Be our representative, our public relations man," he said bluntly. "We'll send you all over the world as our emissary. You'll get 20% of whatever connections and business you bring in. And we tend to attract a lot of business, so, how much you earn is up to you."

This sounded like an amazing opportunity doing what I already knew

I did well. I was delighted. I couldn't wait to tell my mother. Although I could never tell her exactly what type of business venture this was, I excitedly told her about how much money I'd be making. I was so confident she'd be pleased.

"No," her response was visceral. She knew immediately from the figures that it wasn't all above board. "I don't want you getting a penny from this. It's dishonest or illegal. If I ever find out you're doing something like this, I will disown you. The whole world will know you are dead to me."

I was surprised, and I feel like I should have been more hurt and broken than I was. But I trusted and loved my mother with all my heart, and she made sense. I returned to the don and declined the offer. He simply laughed.

"We knew it was a long shot," he chuckled. "You are too decent a man. But remember, if you're ever in trouble, we've got your back."

12

The Devil's prettiest trick is to persuade us he doesn't exist!

Charles Baudelaire

I had begun attending church regularly with an Assemblies of God congregation by this point, still searching for some direction for my life. I never really liked the worship and singing. I got tired and bored. I loved the speakers, though. The topics, the delivery, and the rapport they built with the congregation was inspiring. They were always well-researched, and I could feel them deposit more and more knowledge into me. I picked up public speaking tips from them, too and added them to my arsenal.

One Sunday evening, as I sat there, tuned out of worship, I reflected on my life and career. Why did I have so much trouble keeping hold of success? I had a decent business and good connections. I felt like I was proficient and good at what I did. But it was as if some unseen power was always trying to take away everything I worked for. My earnings seemed to slide out of my hands, like water. Financial situations beyond my control always seemed to pop up. Whether it was friend in need or a cheating acquaintance, something demanded attention. No matter how much money I made, I never seemed to be able to save anything.

The speaker started his sermon, and I was interested to discover that it was an American guest speaker. He was talking about spiritual warfare, and I was hooked.

"We do not wrestle with flesh and blood, but against the principalities of the spirit," he said. He quoted scripture before continuing to speak. "Human trauma in life has a spiritual or demonic link, and deliverance through prayer from spiritual strongholds is necessary for true healing to take place. Demonic activities can bring mental or emotional breakdown, chronic sickness, financial insufficiency, barrenness…"

He continued to list ailments, but my mind was already reeling. Was my continual financial insufficiency a spiritual problem? Was it the devil's handiwork to teach me a lesson because I had refused a well-paid offer? Logically, I couldn't understand how demons could be responsible for everything bad. After all, it's easy to blame the devil for shortcomings rather than personal moral failure or character immaturity. But the speaker then made a poignant statement, breaking into my thoughts.

"The devil brings the lust of the flesh, the lust of the eyes, and the pride of life." He then quoted Ephesians 6:10-20:

> *Finally, be strong in the Lord and in his mighty power. Put on the full armour of God so that you can take your stand against the devil's schemes. For our struggle is not against flesh and blood, but against the rulers, against the authorities, against the powers of this dark world and against the spiritual forces of evil in the heavenly realms. Therefore put on the full armour of God, so that when the day of evil comes, you may be able to stand your ground, and after you have done everything, to stand. Stand firm then, with the belt of truth buckled around your waist, with*

the breastplate of righteousness in place, and with your feet fitted with the readiness that comes from the gospel of peace. In addition to all this, take up the shield of faith, with which you can extinguish all the flaming arrows of the evil one. Take the helmet of salvation and the sword of the Spirit, which is the word of God. And pray in the Spirit on all occasions with all kinds of prayers and requests. With this in mind, be alert and always keep on praying for all the saints.

"Take heed, church," he continued. "Be prepared at all times by putting on the armour of God. Keep praying in the power of the Holy Spirit and remain alert. Expect spiritual conflict, and it will be your key to success."

He went on to talk about the importance of fact, faith, and feeling, specifically in that order. He said that the Bible gives us the facts that activate our faith, and if we submit our feelings to those two, feelings will take care of themselves. If we get the order wrong and start with our feelings, we will be as unstable because feelings are by nature unstable, and don't provide a strong foundation. Facts never change; feelings do in a moment.

I confess I was awed by his knowledge and presentation, even in my scepticism. He related his topic to everyday life and experiences, using personal stories that helped me make sense of it. I thought back to my supernatural experience at my cousin's seemingly haunted house. I wondered if I was under spiritual attack for refusing to join and work for a "dark church".

Christianity was gradually becoming more and more real to me; it was helping me see things, my life, people around me differently. Perhaps spiritual attacks were responsible for addictions and diseases, and that's why people felt restored by prayer. But then, what about healing that happened in other religions? At this point, I didn't accept that Christianity was the only way to know God. I simply concluded that there were multiple paths to redemption and healing both spiritual and physical ailments. Through all this, I had to navigate between my head and my heart, trying hard to reconcile what each part of me said was right.

*   *   *

Following this sermon on spiritual warfare, I became very interested in the demonic realm and how the devil operated. I was on the lookout for meetings or seminars where ex-Satanists would be speaking. I was just so curious! Surprisingly, the wait wasn't long. After putting out the ask, I was invited to a seminar on the works of the devil, where people who used to belong to the dark creed were giving testimonies. It was one of the most unusual yet interesting seminars I've ever been to.

The first speaker opened by saying that the devil's greatest trick is making people believe that he doesn't exist.

"There are a lot of lies floating around about the devil," he said. "The fact that he's the opposite of God, a man in a red suit with horns, a pointy tail and a pitchfork. People say he is the ruler of hell and, arguably the most toxic lie is that 'the devil made you do it'." I was interested. Had I not just been thinking about the futility of blaming all our shortcomings on the devil? I leaned forward, ready to hear the rest of his speech.

"The devil is out to deceive, torment, and destroy us," he continued. "At the core of his being, he wants to keep us from the truth because he knows that the truth, the Word of God, will set us free. He starts in the mind, where most of the warfare begins. Our thoughts are the main battleground. Only when he conquers that part of us can he move into other areas of our lives as well."

In other words, the devil's main agenda is to drop a thought into our minds. Once we accept it, we act upon it. Then it becomes a stranglehold, and people are trapped. Our own thoughts become a vice that keeps us from the truth, and we make ourselves sick over them. One lie from the devil can keep us in a constant state of suffering, torment, or bitterness. And it lasts as long as we permit it. Thoughts like "you're not good enough," "you'll never make it to heaven," "you're useless, worthless, broken so what's the use of trying" are toxic. They bring fear and condemnation, taking root in our mind as we hear or speak them. Eventually, what was once an external voice becomes our own, and we take ownership of ideas that were never ours to begin with. Our family life suffers, as do our relationships, and our faith. Ultimately, the devil comes to steal, kill, and destroy spiritual lives.

After he finished speaking, two other people gave their testimonies. They both used to be part of the devil's kingdom and spoke behind a white screen to hide their identities. The first person was a gifted musician, lured by fame and money. He said everything was exciting when he first joined. He was thriving. But soon, he realised his gifts were luring young people into sex, drugs, and mental problems. His college concerts sucked students into a world of glamour and showbiz. Young girls were promised modelling and acting opportunities and would eventually fall to substance abuse, selling their bodies to fund the lifestyle. People were being possessed by evil spirits, and he was a key player in it all.

He spoke about how he wanted to get out of the lifestyle, and the only thing that gave him hope was Jesus. He told us that the blood of Jesus washed him from all his sins and severed the attachment with the enemy. He'd been spreading the word of God through music ever since. His stories reminded me of moments in my childhood, possessions I'd witnessed, interacting with mediums… it felt like it all linked together.

The next speaker was even more intense. He was commanded by the devil to destroy churches and pastors through violence. Churches everywhere, he said, had witches and devil worshippers residing within them for the sole purpose of destroying God's work. Finally, during one particular confrontation with a priest, rather than killing him, he found himself filled with the Holy Spirit. He was set free from bondage and, through plenty of prayer and love, had been forever changed.

I got goosebumps listening to these testimonies. The strength and power of prayer and blood of Christ was evident. In my still naive mind, I couldn't actually comprehend the depth of meaning of this, but I knew it meant something. I could feel it.

The final speaker concluded the evening by talking about discouragement and how we must be careful not to give into it. I learned that if we are being insulted or humiliated, to remember that God put us there for a reason, and we will surface in an appropriate time for His glory. When the devil tries to delay this future, he is wasting his time. God has planted a kingdom seed in every one of us, and it will manifest when we seek Him and under His guidance. The devil will always lie to us and try to tell us we are not worthy of God's love. But we need to remember we are created in the image and likeness of God. He cares for us so much that he sent his only Son to die for us on the cross and that whoever believes in Him will not perish but have everlasting life.

Something within me flickered to life upon hearing this. It was still difficult for me to grasp the concept of God having a human son that was sent to earth to die. But my spirit was stirred. What struck me the most in all this was the transformative power of God. Someone hopeless can blossom into someone amazing who draws people and positive energy to them, guiding, directing, and protecting those around them.

My main question at this point was why did an omnipotent,

omnipresent, and omniscient God have to do any of this to save making from sin? My understanding of sin had Hindu roots. Hinduism has no eternal hell, Satan, or intrinsic evil. According to my grandfather, sin and suffering was part of human life, and we were not afflicted by anyone but ourselves. Karma is a big part of Hindu doctrine, stating that what we put out into the world, we will reap, and it will affect the next life we have. We must go through a seven stage process to exonerate any trespasses we commit.

After the event, I asked a Christian preacher, "Can you please explain the difference between karma and sin?"

"Karma is a Hindu concept that believes sin doesn't affect the relationship with God," he explained. "Whether karma is good or bad makes no difference to the fact that we are unconditionally extended from the oneness of God. In Christianity, sin *does* affect our relationship with God. It alienates us from Him. The Christian God is a personal one, and he can forgive us of our sins through Jesus Christ."

I still didn't quite understand the Christian view of sin. There was so much to take in from this seminar, a whirlwind of information. The concepts of heaven, hell, sin, Satan, death, salvation, karma, and reincarnations fought for attention in my mind.

I continued attending meetings, always armed with questions. I was still trying to figure out which voice to listen to—heart or mind? Most of the time, I felt like there was no God, but then I would hear incredible testimonies of people being transformed, and I was momentarily swayed. But then the logical mind would take over again, and I went back to unbelief. I felt like a pendulum swinging back and forth.

Not long after meeting these reformed ex-Satanists, a few Christian friends invited me to an Evangelical Union meeting, promising I could enrich my Christian knowledge and faith. What could I say, but, "Yes, please!"

*　　*　　*

The next day, I made my way to large city flat. It was full of young, smiling people, snacks laid out creating a warm and welcoming environment. Everyone introduced themselves to me, which was quite nice. I felt part of the family almost instantly. The meeting began with singing and worship, and I was reminded of the music lessons from my childhood. The melody was just so full of joy and freedom, it was so beautiful to see young people having so much *fun* in a Bible study group.

Soon after worship, the leader began to speak. He looked too young to be a preacher, I thought.

"I'm just going to clear up some conceptions about religion," he began, almost flippantly. "Have you ever wondered if there is a God? Have you wondered how we can know Him?"

He had a strangely sarcastic tone, as if anyone who thought these questions was a moron. I didn't like it. It was condescending, and suddenly it wasn't just the pleasant music lessons from my primary school that this meeting emulated. Suddenly, I was a young boy again, and the teachers were talking down to me. This young man's public speaking skills were not on the same level as the preachers I had witnessed at other churches. It was as if he was using someone else's sermon and just adapting it to himself. There was no passion or humility in his voice. He kept checking his notes, looking underprepared. I began to tune out and was set on never coming back.

But then he said, "Have you ever asked yourself if you should follow what you think is right or what you feel is right?" I tuned straight back in again. I had been quick to dismiss his talk, but here he was, asking the question that had been bothering me for weeks.

"Can you imagine," he continued, still in that awful tone, "we have so many educated people, and nobody has ever asked this question." He mentioned the French philosopher Rousseau, who had concluded that one has to have a parameter against which their beliefs must be tested. We can believe whatever we want and *feel* that we are right, but if the facts contradict that, we are wrong. Despite the condescension in the man's voice, I was fascinated. The parameter he was talking about in this case was the Bible. But, I thought, what about other religions and their scriptures? Surely, they become the parameters for others? But then, who is right? I had a lot to think about, but no answers from this meeting.

Soon afterward, the same group of acquaintances invited me to visit a ship, the MV Doulos, which was in port nearby for a few weeks. It was the biggest floating library and bookshop in the world that aimed to bring knowledge and hope by sharing the message of God whenever possible. They expected thousands of visitors every day. It offered over 5,000 titles, giving many visitors their first insight into educational Christian literature.

I tagged along with the group and met a girl volunteering on the ship who had converted from Hinduism. She was a very passionate and persuasive Christian and took me around as a tour guide, showing me the titles and Bibles that might interest me. One of the books, *I Dared to Call Him Father*, chronicled a Muslim woman, Bilquis Sheikh's journey from Islam to Christianity. That was the book I bought.

Raised in Islam with wealth and prestige, Sheikh had faced hardship as an adult, which, combined with spiritual dreams, led her to explore Christianity. When she finally accepted a commitment to Jesus, she found personal freedom.

I was hooked on every word of her story. I had never read anything like this before, and I couldn't put it down. It was so inspiring. But it didn't quite answer the questions I held still in my heart. How can Christ be the only right God and the others all wrong? It was a good start, but there was still more to uncover.

* * *

I visited that ship many times while it was in town, buying plenty of books on each visit. There were also tapes that went into detail on various cults and how they operated. They were quite interesting, showing the reality of sacrifices, financial and sexual exploitation, and cheap labor. I learned much from this resource.

MV Doulos also hosted seminars and workshops where people told their own story about how they found Jesus as their Lord and Saviour. The speakers were from all over the world, different races, religious origins, and backgrounds. But they all had one thing in common—the love and grace of Jesus had transformed their lives. I listened intently, soaking in the joy they expressed.

I loved that they were also very open to questions.

"Will the people who have never heard of Jesus go to hell? How were people saved before Christ's resurrection?" I asked one of the speakers.

He explained to me that God doesn't expect people to respond to something they've never heard of. But the Bible tells us that all people are accountable to know that God exists. Romans 1:20 says, "For since the creation of the world, God's invisible qualities—his eternal power and divine nature—have been clearly seen, being understood from what has been made, so that men are without excuse." In other words, the sheer complexity of the world around us tells us that there is a God. And sure, science can explain much about what we experience, but deep down, everything works too perfectly for it to have been born of pure chance. That was his stance.

He also told me that everyone knows we are sinners on some level. No one can claim perfect innocence because there are laws and rules in place that we have all broken. There's also the fact that all of humanity has a moral compass within their hearts that intrinsically knows that the most basic sins, like theft or lying, are wrong. How we respond to these two apparently self-evident truths—the existence of God in nature's complexity and our own instinctual knowledge of sin—is the crucial point.

The speaker emphasised that salvation is founded on God's grace, not our works—we don't become righteous by performing rituals. His grace is given through Jesus' death and resurrection, and nothing we do can change that. He is the way, the truth and the life. No one comes to the Father but through Him. Once saved, we are commissioned to tell others about Him, to go to the ends of the earth to declare His gospel.

This was a pretty uncompromising point of view. And yet, when the speaker spoke about humbling ourselves before God, I found I was listening keenly. It was a concept that hit a note for me. But it wasn't a comfortable note. I could feel fear and insecurity holding me back from total acceptance of this idea.

*   *   *

I was visiting many religious meetings, as many different faiths as I could during that time. I learned a lot of different views about the concept and nature of God. Some people believe there are many gods, that there is one, or even that everything is god. Everyone I encountered had differing views of humanity, too, but seemed to agree that we are all made up of body, soul (mind and will), and spirit. There was a lot take to take in with so many religions bombarding my mind. It's perhaps no surprise that I was struggling with the idea that only one of these could be right. All of them clearly had power over their congregations. Their members were all dedicated and determined.

I met people who were willing to fight, kill, and die for their religion. But I wanted to see someone really live for their religion, practice their religion in its purest form. From what I saw, a lot of followers were only there out of childhood indoctrination, fear, desperation, tradition, comfort… anything but true devotion. What I did unravel though, was an answer to my question about the greatest power a man can have: *control over other people's minds*. Charismatic religious leaders had an ability to command their followers through thought, and I witnessed it regularly. They were domineering, and they used fear and intimidation to keep people's thoughts and behaviour in check. People unquestioningly absorbed what they were told to believe, and it was what directed all their actions even outside of religious life. Which led me to another conclusion—that humanity's greatest desire is not just to follow God, but to *be* God, at least to be Gods in the here and now, on earth.

*   *   *

During the first Gulf War, I was traveling to the Indian state of Gujarat. The train took two days to get to the capital, and I was lucky enough to be invited to the festival of Navratri. Literally meaning "nine nights," it is one of the greatest Hindu festivals, where people dance and dress beautifully, a celebration of how good's triumph over evil. Durga, Lakshmi, and Saraswati are worshipped as different manifestations of *Shakti* (cosmic energy). I was looking forward to it.

Midway through the journey, the train stopped, and the passengers were evacuated. I found out that the Gulf War had caused a fuel shortage, so only a few trains could run. Three trains were cancelled that day, and all the passengers were flooding the platform. It was hot and chaotic, people swarming like bees. It was an agonising eight hours until another train finally came. Three trains worth of people pushing their way onto the new train, fighting for a seat. It was pandemonium. There were children crying and women screaming.

I ran for my life, determined to make this train. The compartment was full but I managed to find the edge of a seat. But then I saw a woman struggling with her small child and thought it better to offer it to her. I stood in the compartment, breathing in the fumes of people pressing in on all sides. I was feeling claustrophobic and crushed.

It was even worse when railway officers came through, checking our tickets. As I watched, I realised they were falsely accusing a lot of tickets of being invalid just to get money off us. The injustice made my blood boil. Earlier that day, the ticket checkers assured me, as well as the other passengers, that our tickets would still be valid even though it was a different train because of the special circumstances. But here they were, ready to use their little bit of power to rip us off. People around me began to notice what was happening and were getting restless. I was ready for confrontation.

"Is this what humanity has come to?" I said, loudly. "Where you exploit the weak because you can?" Some people around me nodded their approval, but, for the most part, they were terrified of how the situation would unfold. They were worried they might get kicked off the service. But I was determined to see this through to the end. I made another attempt to gain support.

"Can you believe this?" I continued. "We are traveling to the birthplace of Mahatma Gandhi, the father of our nation who gave up his life for honesty, integrity, and freedom. Yet the people who are supposed to protect us are using their power to torment us. We have to do something or people like this will never learn their lesson." I could hear the officers approaching. A loud cry from a woman came from behind me. The abuses of officers seemed to be escalating.

From what I could gather, the woman was breastfeeding as the officers passed, so she did not immediately respond to their demands for money. As a consequence, one of the officers called her a prostitute, and she started shouting in retaliation. Her husband heard her yells and approached the situation. He was in fact a senior officer in the Central Reserve Police Force. And that's when all hell broke loose. He started yelling at the railway officers, promising to get them fired and jailed on corruption and extortion charges. Terrified, the officers scurried away, and everything suddenly settled down. Power only answered to more power.

The train regained some sense of sanity and peace after that. Many people were sharing seats and sleeping space, but I noticed a man by himself in a sleeping area. I approached to him and started a conversation. I discovered that he was a Regional Director of a Christian church in his area. I told him about my spiritual journey, the things I had discovered thus far, and how they had prompted more and more questions.

He told me he was doing great work in the region, that he had earned much power and prestige through it. He told me about all the connections he made and how he wanted to travel the world and meet important people. To be frank, he had a terrible attitude, arrogant and grasping. He started tucking into his dinner, eating in a horribly sloppy way without regard for those around him. Fortunately, he soon turned over and went to sleep, precluding further conversation. He reminded me of some of the religious leaders who had turned me off—hypocrites incapable of embodying the "love thy neighbour" principle.

Meanwhile, in the same section, there was an old father and his son who asked me if I wanted to join them for dinner. When I declined, they offered me space in their cot even though they had already given some space to someone else. I knew if I joined, they would not be comfortable, so I politely declined again. However, I was touched by their compassion and generosity. I found out that they were of Jain origins. I didn't know much about this religion, but their integrity and genuine spirit inspired me to seek out Jainism, and I ended up actively practicing for the next three years as I continued my spiritual exploration. That's the power of sincerity and generosity.

*   *   *

But before I had a chance to learn more about Jainism, I found myself battling a less heartfelt religious group. The day after the train fiasco, I finally reached the capital city of Gujrat. After lunch, I explored the area and found myself in the main city centre. I saw a large group of people outside a building, handing out leaflets.

"Welcome! Welcome! Welcome to the mother's paradise!" A young man exclaimed, holding a leaflet out to me.

"Who are you talking about?" I asked, puzzled.

"My friend, you are a lucky person," he replied. "Mother has called you, you are in the right place at the right time. This is a meditation seminar where we call upon Mother, the supreme guru. She will appear to us, bless us, heal us, and solve all our problems." I was curious, even though I felt deep down that this was a con. But I was ready to challenge and smash another cult, so I accepted.

The hall was huge and filled to capacity, about 500 people. The lights dimmed, and loud, hypnotic music filled the air. A voice boomed through the speakers.

"Take deep breaths and relax your body. Let your body go loose and limp. Let the universal white light surround you. Breathe deeply in and out. Let your mind relax. Let all your worries go, your tension go, let everything go! Surrender your mind and body to the supreme white light. Relax. You are safe, for mother is coming to embrace you. She knows the burden you are carrying, the pain you are holding in your heart, the struggles you are going through! Set your ego free! Do not hold on to any thoughts; just let yourself go! Inhale and now exhale! Inhale and now exhale! Inhale and now exhale!"

I kept my eyes open the whole time, more intent on observing than participating. There was an American couple circling the room with torches, making sure everyone had their eyes closed. As they approached my row, I quickly shut my eyes and feigned obedience. In that moment, I heard a scream. Not an ordinary shout, but a piercing scream that impaled my heart.

"Mother has come! Mother has come!" a woman repeated again and again, her voice shrill. Then another voice sounded from the other side of the hall, just as loud and terrifying as this one. The screaming rippled across the room and soon, people throughout were crying hysterically, rolling on the floor. Some were tearing their clothes, some banging their hands and feet on the floor. The chaos and mayhem was deeply unsettling, and it left me uncomfortable, my heart heavy. Painful memories from my past were stirred up by this negative energy. Sadness was surfacing along with anger and frustration. I was angry because of the clear hypnotism and manipulation that this cult was using. I was helpless and couldn't do anything about it.

The scene lasted for over an hour until it came time to share testimonies of what Mother had done for the people. Some people said they had a vision of being rich, getting married or healed. The most bizarre testimonies were those that claimed Mother had told them in advance about income tax raids in order to protect them and their finances. It was obvious that people only joined this group in the hopes of attaining all their worldly desires, material gains.

Then came the offering. A huge chest was placed on the stage, and money came pouring in from all over the hall. As I stepped outside, an elder of the group confronted me, knowing I was an outsider. With an eager expression, he asked what I thought of the experience. I told him bluntly that I wasn't stupid—this was just brainwashing to manipulate money out of people. The man's face changed, and other elders drew near to support him after hearing my loud voice. The American man from earlier heard the commotion and approached.

"Are there any problems here?" he asked. "We do not like unwanted people coming here and disrupting the meeting. What's your problem?"

"This is a con," I said hotly. "You're brainwashing people, and I know enough not to be part of this foolishness. You give empty promises so that people can give you money and time for your own selfish gain." I could tell he was surprised by how fluent I was in English. He wasn't expecting someone like me to challenge him.

"All I have witnessed today," I continued, boldly, "is mass hypnotism, exploiting gullible people for what little they have." Upon realising that he was not going to wear me down, the American called upon his sergeant-at-arms and told me to direct my questions to him instead. I was introduced to a man named Suresh. He was a young, fierce man full of zeal and enthusiasm, ready to convert me. My love for the game and challenges awoke. We walked and talked away from the tense and hostile environment that we were in.

"So why did you join the group?" I cut right to the point once we were out of earshot of the rest of the elders.

Suresh told me an unexpected tale, of feeling suicidal after the heartbreak of lost love. "In my brokenness," he said, "I met someone from here who told me about Mother. Someone who could solve my problems and break through all my burdens? Sounded good to me. I've been here ever since, dedicating my life to this place, free of charge." He went on to say he'd found a job through friends he met here, and that he was ready to repay the favour by helping to spread the word about the group's helping and healing power.

The initial hostility I felt from him melted away as he told his story. As he opened up about his life, I felt a familiar friendly warmth. I told him that I had spent a lot of time studying cults and asked if he thought this group had any of the characteristics of cults. After some discussion, we agreed that this group had some trademarks of a cult. Members were unquestioningly committed to their leader, and doubts were discouraged and sometimes punished. Mind-altering practices were carried out regularly with members feeling special and elite. Shame and guilt were used to manipulate behaviour. There was also a degree of separation from family and friends that were outside the group and a focus on bringing in new members and money. It was sad. Members found their way here, hoping for release. They wanted to be freed from burdens and pain, ready to commit to Mother, only to find themselves in bondage of a different form. The worst part was, they didn't even realise they were enslaved.

Suddenly, I realised the last question on my list had been definitively answered. *The greatest treasure a man can have is freedom.*

"For what shall it profit a man, if he shall gain the whole world and lose his own soul?" The Bible verse (Mark 8:36) spilled out of my mouth before I even realised what was happening. I was shocked at myself and confused. While I had read this verse before, it wasn't exactly at the forefront of my mind ready for me to call on. But there it was. Suresh was both surprised and fascinated. I invited him to a meal in my hotel to continue our conversation.

As we ate, he burst into tears and poured his heart out to me. He told me about all his disappointments, his shortcomings and setbacks, the heartache, and, above all, his lost love. He found meaning in the cult when nothing seemed to matter anymore. He dived headfirst into it in an attempt to erase the past and drift peacefully into a better future. After an emotional dinner, we parted hoping to meet again in the future.

I felt sad for the man and was frustrated that I couldn't offer more than a few encouraging words and book recommendations. He clearly loved the woman deeply and was still hurting. Our conversation revealed that he was basically using the cult group as a bandage on an open wound, and he realised he needed to focus more on self-development and his career.

We parted as new friends, but my quest for truth was still not over. I remembered the father and son on the train who were practising Jainism. In spite of the ease with which I had deployed a Bible verse to help Suresh, the memory of the humanity and generosity on the train ride held a wonderful allure. It seemed like a good place to go from here, and with that, I focused my time on understanding the religion.

*   *   *

Jainism is one of the oldest religions in the world. Adherents follow the teachings of 24 prophets known as Tirthankaras, to whom they also pray. They believe in a multi-layered universe, which contains a series of heavens and hells, and where the most liberated souls reside in the Supreme Abode. Like Hindus, they believed that everyone is bound by karma, but there is no "good karma" for Jains. There is simply an accumulation of all evil deeds stacked up for each individual. There were traces of Buddhism in there too, with *Moksha* being similar to a state of enlightenment where one breaks the cycle of reincarnation through asceticism.

The three general principles, or *ratnas*, that define Jain life are right faith, right knowledge, and right action. They were called to a life of non-violence (*Ahisma*), truth (*Satya*), honesty (*Asteya*—more specifically, not stealing), monogamy (*Brahma-charya*) and detachment from material things, people, and places (*Aparigraha*). I agreed with these principles and thought they produced good quality people—like the father and son on the train. I was drawn in by their strength of character and started implementing these principles in my life.

I started with having only two boiled vegetarian meals a day. I also stopped using perfumes and luxury cosmetics. I simplified my sleeping habits, using only a sheet on the floor, even fasting for 21 days. The last task proved very difficult as the lack of energy made me dizzy, and I blacked out a few times. I became very weak, and a doctor told me if I continued this way, I would die. That's when the fast ended.

What I gathered from this experience was that we could find the will to do extremely difficult things if we trust ourselves. All these things that I had done made me feel imbued with a sense of that power over myself, a power of *personal* mind control. I could detach myself emotionally from anything and anyone if I just willed my mind to do so. I believed it would ultimately purify my spirit and free me from bondage.

But ultimately, all I really wanted, was a relationship with a *higher* power. Someone or something I could communicate with outside of myself. Yet all depictions of God I had learned about felt remote, and practices I had participated in seemed designed to keep Him at a remove. I wasn't ready to settle for this. I needed that personal connection, so I kept searching.

*   *   *

Even as I explored the very extremes of my own mind's abilities through Jainism, I was also a regular attendee to Christian meetings all over the city. I was hungry to learn more, casting as wide a net as possible. The welcoming atmosphere at church was constant, no matter how often I was there. At one of the meetings, someone suggested that I read a book called *Death of a Guru* by Rabi Maharaj. As a book-lover, I had no problem with this and picked up a copy as soon as I could.

It was the remarkable life story of Maharaj, a former yogi. The story seemed so familiar and close to my own life and upbringing, I was genuinely fascinated. He was born from a long line of Brahmin priests and gurus and trained as a yogi from the age of five. His world was filled with spirits, gods, and occult powers, and he was obliged from that young age to give his attention to all of these areas.

Maharaj's father was a Head Priest, making him a powerful man in the community. He was dedicated to yoga and seeking the true self. He died mysteriously and suddenly, his body given to Agni, the god of fire. That strong mantle of leadership was now passed onto Rabi, who, like his father, was also revered almost as a god, even as a very young man.

Rabi felt a mystical union with each god he worshipped as he sat before the altar. In moments of deep meditation, in a state of Yogic trance, he often found himself alone with Shiva the Destroyer, with whom he would speak. Yet in his studies, Rabi became overly aware that the nation of his religion was incredibly poor. How could this be when so many people were practising yoga and improving their karma? It didn't make sense to him.

One day, he saw a menacingly thick snake making its way towards him, its eyes intently staring into his. He was paralysed with fear. In an inexplicable moment, he yelled a name he never thought he would rely on.

"Jesus, help me!"

To his complete astonishment, the snake dropped to the ground and wriggled away into the underbrush.

For some years Rabi had considered that God was the creator of the universe, not just part of it, an idea that contradicted the Hindu belief that God was one with creation. He couldn't marry these two versions of God, and struggled internally with understanding what was right. He began questioning everything else he knew. Were the gods and spirits he invoked good or bad? How could he know that the bliss he sought wasn't an illusion? In retrospect, he knew the Lord was preparing his heart.

Even though he was conflicted, Rabi continued blessing people as a Hindu priest and continued practicing yoga, hoping to find clarity through the practice. He was afraid to open his heart to Jesus because of his Hindu community and family. And yet Rabi saw for himself how full of joy Christians were during worship in contrast to the dark, stoic nature of his own Hindu practices.

One day, when he was reaching forward to touch a poor widow, he heard an authoritative and firm voice.

"You are not God, Rabi!" His arm froze midair. He abandoned the woman and went to his room, seeking God. It was a defining moment in his life. The old Rabi died and was born anew in Christ. He walked in a newfound freedom, unbound from the desire to be a God himself, delivered from all evil.

This book gave me much to think on.

*   *   *

The first time I met Jonathan Maraj, a pastor who was born to a Hindu family, I was at the Evangelical Union group. He was a preacher and I loved hearing him speak with such passion and conviction. He was great storyteller, his testimony pulling me into his experience rather than just recounting it. He had grown up unwanted, his birth considered a bad omen by his family. He spent his young life full of anger and resentment. He found redemption in Christ, his spirit and heart transformed through the power of God. He had the whole hall hooked on his every word, dropping fire on the congregation.

He then explained that we were all born inherently sinful, falling short of God's glory and that we needed Jesus' redemption. It was so different to what I learned growing up. Hinduism taught that it was bad karma to do the wrong thing, not that we were born sinful.

Me? I thought. A born sinner? At first, I was livid. I thought he got it wrong, so, when the meeting ended, I approached him and demanded an explanation. I told him about all my principles, that I was a generally good person, that I didn't smoke or drink. I was offended that I was accused of being a sinner. He smiled at me with such charm, humility, and kindness that it was difficult to stay offended.

He explained to me that the biblical concept of sin is disobedience to God. And in that respect, we've all fallen short of His glory. His gift to us of free will makes it even more meaningful when we choose to use our lives for good, and more tragic when we don't. The purpose of life is to live in close communion with God.

"Brother Sanjay," he said, each syllable imbued with love. "The only way to get salvation is turn away from sin and accept Jesus as your Lord and Saviour." He then asked me if he could pray for me and spoke the most amazing words over my life. He asked God to touch my heart and draw me near to Him, to reveal Himself and His love to me.

I was blown away by the humility in this man. He taught me that the Bible is a historically accurate document that has been confirmed with archaeological investigations, while simultaneously being infallible scriptures that reveal the mind of God. I was also interested to find that most of the thousands of prophecies that appear in the Bible have been fulfilled. The Bible was becoming more and more credible to me.

"Brother Jonathan, what does it actually mean to be a Christian?" I asked quite directly.

He replied with a smile, "To be Christian is to know Christ and to make Christ known."

"Brother, I'm sorry but can you please give me a practical answer that I can understand?"

"It means to be the best son, the best student, the best friend, the best employee. It means to be a man of God, honest, full of integrity and humility. It means to love everyone just the way God loved us." He quoted Philippians 1:21: "For to me, to live is Christ and to die is gain."

"So what would you do if someone broke into your house and threatened your family?" I tried to probe deeper, get some insight into his inner self by asking him tough questions and reading his reactions. His face flushed at the idea of his family being harmed, but his answer was still civilised.

"I can't say that I know for sure how I would act. But I do know that I would protect my family with my life."

He went on to tell me how a gang once threatened his life but he wasn't afraid. They would be doing him a favour by sending him to his heavenly Father. I was touched by his honesty. The more I listened to him, the more questions I had.

"Brother Jonathan," I said, "you are a great man and I am deeply touched by everything you've said and done. But how can I trust a God that I haven't seen? How can all the other religions be wrong and only Jesus be right?"

"The Bible is clear about it," he said patiently. He handed me his own personal Bible and urged me to remember that Jesus loves us all. "Get immersed in His word, and you will soon discover how amazing the God we serve is. He is a God who never leaves you nor forsakes you, one who loves you unconditionally and a God that never fails. I could fail you and others could fail you, but Jesus never will. I am not perfect so never worship me."

Another man who rejected any desire to be a God himself.

I noticed just how loving he was in answering my questions, full of patience and kindness. I was reminded of the camp leader from years before that listened just as intently. It seemed to be a recurring theme among genuine Christians. He touched my heart that day. Our friendship blossomed following this first conversation, and I went on a Christian camp that he was speaking at. He said things so simply but they had so much power behind them. Even though he would be preaching all day, he still found time to sit and talk with me late into the night, answering my questions until other elders whisked him away.

"There is no breaking God's law by different degrees," he said to me one night, "if you miss the mark by one or fifty, you've still failed the test. Jesus was crucified for all sin, and He is the only way to salvation." Again, the beliefs I grew up on were challenged. I had assumed all religions led to heaven and the details didn't matter. As long as people were doing good things, it would be okay. I still struggled to accept that I was a sinner. And I still struggled to put my full faith in this Christian God.

*   *   *

The more time I spent in Christian circles, the more I heard the expression "born again." Though I had myself experienced moments of spiritual clarity, I wasn't exactly sure what the phrase meant. I wanted to know more about this idea, specifically from Hindus that converted to Christianity. Not long after making the request, God delivered once more.

I met a group of Hindus who had been born again who came from very affluent backgrounds and were well educated, which wasn't what I was expecting. But each one had a powerful story to tell.

A young man named Kaushik was a troublemaker in his boarding school. He often ran away or snuck out of the dorm with his friends. He had a smart mouth but one of the Christian teachers invited him to a prayer meeting whenever he could. Of course, Kaushik never bothered. One day, Kaushik was climbing a hill when he slipped, fell and broke his leg. It was the most painful experience in his life. He felt isolated by the physical hurt, but the teacher would always visit and console him. When Kaushik was in pain during his rehabilitation, the teacher came in and asked Kaushik if she could pray for him. Although he didn't believe in prayer, he was in so much pain that he agreed to anything that might help.

"Kaushik," she began, "do you believe that Jesus can heal you?"

Despite everything he thought he knew and believed, Kaushik found himself blurting out a loud "Yes!"

"Kaushik…in the name of Jesus, walk!" Kaushik felt a surge of power run through his body, almost like an electric shock as she said the words. He got up and not just walked but ran and ran and ran, tears flowing down his face, screaming with joy. He accepted Jesus in his life that day, but it came at a price. His parents disowned him for it. But he continued on his newfound path.

Coming from a Hindu background myself, I understood the singular pain of parental rejection all too well. I was also amazed that this young man had the courage to walk away from all the luxuries he had in life to love and serve God.

Another man spoke of being so deep in Kali worship that he almost killed himself offering blood to her. His wife left him, and he was suicidal when a pastor introduced him to Jesus. Like Kaushik, his life was immediately transformed, and he felt dark spirits leave him as soon as he reached out and prayed to God. He felt a warmth and a peace he didn't know was possible and he knew he had found truth. And also like Kaushik, his parents opposed this conversion. He kept faith, and God provided for him, giving him everything he needed day by day. His wife was restored to him, food was always taken care of, and, even though his parents didn't convert, his mum was healed of what could have been a deadly illness.

I asked him what it meant to be born again and his response was quite interesting.

He told me that, while Hinduism teaches that we can only realise God through self-purification and a complete change of consciousness, being born again in a biblical sense doesn't rely on rituals or symbolic gestures; simply believing in God and allowing Him to transform us into new creations was enough. He showed me the passage John 3:3-5 that reads "Jesus replied, 'Very truly I tell you, no one can see the kingdom of God unless they are born again.' 'How can someone be born when they are old?' Nicodemus asked. 'Surely they cannot enter a second time into their mother's womb to be born!' Jesus answered, 'Very truly I tell you, no one can enter the kingdom of God unless they are born of water and the Spirit.'"

Hearing stories like these was truly inspiring. I noticed that each person talked about having a personal relationship with God. They willingly gave up everything for Him, were willing to die for their faith. I had finally found the true devotees of Christianity, and it was thrilling. They were also learned individuals who answered all my questions with examples and evidence rooted in the Bible.

As I met and talked with more and more Hindu converts, I heard stories of miraculous healing where diseases completely disappeared after prayer. High caste individuals whose value had hitherto been in their social status were humbled when God revealed Himself during a social downfall. The way one man spoke, you would never know that pride was once his biggest vice. He told me his favourite scripture was Matthew 16:25: "For whosoever will save his life shall lose it; and whosoever will lose his life for my sake shall find it."

And though I couldn't yet understand all the Bible verses, I was building them up in my head, committing many to memory. Talking to these born again Hindus renewed my hope. I knew that the world full of lies, greed, and manipulation lived alongside the one where people gave up everything for truth, love, and service of a loving God. It mirrored the battle between my own heart and mind, and my perception of the society continued to swing like a pendulum between both these worlds.

Part Five

Lamentations

13

We do not receive wisdom,
we must discover it for ourselves after a journey through the wilderness...
Marcel Proust

My grandfather had taught me that Jesus was just another yogi and that he taught people how to be "yoked with God." He believed that Jesus came to India and learned from gurus, preaching his enlightenment to the world—what we now know today as the Gospels. But having gone myself to many Hindu seminars and conferences as well as Christian ones, I saw the same fake devotion I saw in most other religions and cults. People were there for social obligations, financial gain, or power.

I was still unsure that one path to God could be better than any other. If faith in Jesus offered salvation, was that very different from achieving oneness through meditation? Was there a meaningful difference between reincarnation and resurrection? These were tough questions, even for the experts I was talking to. I was left wanting to know more about the effects of Hindu meditation and yoga, to see if there really was a difference between their way and the Jesus way.

I met a man named Mrinal who had joined in a meditation and yoga group in his late teens. After six years, he had a mental breakdown and was in hospital numerous times.

"I felt like I was split in pieces," he told me. "My mind was possessed with voices of many different personalities, and some of them were clairvoyant. I was told of things to happen, and they did. I had many visions, both uplifting and awful. I had out-of-body experiences; my body shook constantly. I was making bad decisions. My emotions were out of control, feeling very high and then feeling very depressed. Sometimes I would fall into sleep and would be suddenly woken up with a jolt. I would see demons and awful atrocities in my visions that I didn't like at all. My work and my family life both got disturbed. I could never build an intimate relationship with anyone. My spiritual seeking had cost me a lot."

I shared a bit of Mrinal's story with a Christian friend I trusted. It troubled me, especially Mrinal saying he couldn't build a relationship with anyone because of his emotional disturbance. Surely the whole point of the yoga and meditation was to achieve a deep relationship with everything! My friend was unsurprised by Mrinal's side effects. He told me that prayer was truly the most powerful way of speaking to God, and that God did not require us to sacrifice our mental or physical wellbeing for Him. All that He asked was our trust and faith, not our blood, sweat, and tears.

Prayer... it sounded like such a docile practice in the Christian faith. So different from the blood offerings that I had grown accustomed to from the Hindu stories. But I was still troubled. I kept coming back to the image of my mother, praying for years and never receiving an answer. If God is one and is everywhere, then why doesn't He answer everyone's prayers?

And, of course, my own experience with prayer at school was terrifying. I had never understood the real meaning of the Lord's Prayer, only saying it to escape pain, so when I heard Christians testify that their prayers were answered, I didn't understand how this could be possible.

I continued to explore prayer through reading and hearing interesting sermons. I was learning that prayer is a multifaceted thing, not a set of words we recite like robots. One pastor in particular gave a fascinating talk on the types of prayer, and using intercession prayers to "bridge the gap" to help people who have lost touch with their faith or who need special assistance. But there was also communion with God, where there's no request made—it's just a chance to spend time experiencing His presence. This reminded me a bit of meditation, but it was so much warmer and more loving.

He explained that three major hindrances to prayer are sin, which distances us from God; selfishness, when we ask for earthly gain instead of spiritual betterment; and an inability to let go of wrongs done to us—a real stumbling block to opening oneself to the eternal love of God.

He even addressed the idea of delayed results. Why does it sometimes take a while before prayers are answered? He proposed that God wants humanity to be one another's answered prayers. It is only through our unity with each other, and ultimately, with God, that we can function the way He intended. And because of our free will and human limitations, not all answers come immediately.

I took many notes at this sermon for future reference. I had been to hundreds of seminars and meetings and speeches at this point. I was intrigued to realise that, no matter how many times I heard the message of the Bible, I never grew bored or tired of hearing it *when the speaker was genuine*. I could see the obstacles to belief in my head and how each was crumbling as I researched Christianity further. I felt like I was on a precipice of truth. But still, where is the proof that God exists, and which manifestation is the real one?

*   *   *

I was beginning to make more Christian friends. One was a preacher who explained to me that faith was not a single step. It was a journey that brought one closer to one's destination. And the progression isn't always linear. It starts with a mental acceptance that there really is a God and that Jesus died on the cross and rose again for our salvation. It moves on to trusting the character, ability and integrity of God, understanding that He loves us all unconditionally. He told me that after these two preliminary steps, he finally accepted Jesus as His Lord and Saviour, was born again and adopted into the Christian family. It was at this point that he learned total dependence on God.

I regularly attended the Assemblies of God church in Calcutta, slowly quenching my thirst for knowledge. The speakers were always brilliant and powerful, yet still humble and approachable and willing to answer my questions. I eventually built quite a strong rapport with the pastors. I soon found myself teaching the things I had learned from these sermons to anyone who would listen, no matter their background.

Some people became bitter and frustrated when I did this, but when I talked about astrology or new age practices, they would listen enthusiastically. It was only the Bible or the church from which they turned.

Then one day, an intellectual friend accused me in public, "You're just being paid by the church to infiltrate other groups to recruit them. You've sold your heart and soul to that church."

I was shocked at the accusation. I was genuinely learning new things and sharing out of my love of knowledge and to improve my public speaking skills. I invited people to see it for themselves, and while some of them said they would join me, they never actually did.

One morning, some friends and I were once again discussing religion when tempers ran high.

"You are a fool to talk about these things!" an acquaintance yelled at me. "The Bible is pure evil, full of murder, rape, and slavery. It is laced with hatred, anger, and genocide. If you think you're so smart, then go find these answers from the church, and see if they have answers for you. I bet you will find all the evil in the Bible and stop talking about it for the rest of your life."

I was taken aback. I hadn't even accepted Jesus, let alone claimed to have all the answers to defend the Bible. I wasn't the type to take it lightly though.

"Yes!" I argued back, "People like you who are low in knowledge compensate with volume. It doesn't take any skill to change a discussion to an argument."

My friends could tell I was angry and knew I shouldn't be tested. They told my accuser to apologise. I calmed down, but I was shaken. How evil was the Bible?

*   *   *

I found material from Christian Apologists that helped me to understand the character of the Christian God. In the Old Testament, God can sometimes appear to be cruel and ruthless, bringing down death and destruction with impunity. That view of God certainly doesn't deserve to be worshipped. But a closer look at the Old Testament actually shows Him to be righteous, patient, and merciful, a mirror of Jesus as found in the New Testament. It is true that the Bible contains graphic stories of sin, evil, and

death. But these are individual moments within a story arc whose themes are love, redemption, and grace. The God of this story metes out freedom, but also justice when that freedom is misused. There are consequences for those who take their freedom for granted and use it to create and perpetuate suffering on Earth. God himself is not evil in visiting his righteousness upon those who do evil.

Even God's command for Abraham to sacrifice his son can be explained. When the scripture is read in its entirety, God clearly never intended for Abraham to follow through. It was a chance for Abraham to show God that he was faithful to him, even at the height of sorrow. And while Abraham was saved the pain of killing his son, God did not hold any of that back for the salvation of humanity. God's own anguish was secondary to His love for humanity.

Amidst this research, I was recommended a book called *The Knowledge of the Holy* by A. W. Tozer. This book became a key part of my perception of God. One quote in particular has stuck with me throughout my life: "What comes into our minds when we think about God is the most important thing about us."[7]

In the book, Tozer informs the reader of a biblical view of God, detailing different attributes as revealed in scripture. He talks about the incomprehensible God—that He is so great, yet we try to limit Him so we can feel more comfortable. The entire book gives evidence for many layers of God—His mercy, justice, the Trinity. It gave me a great understanding of who God is, and it satisfied my worries about whether God could be evil.

But still, my question about Jesus being the *only* way had not been answered. Ten years in convent school taught me that people pray to Mary

---

[7]   Tozer, A.W. (1978) *The Knowledge of the Holy.* New York: HarperCollins (Original work published 1920).

instead of Jesus. Where did that fit? There was much that was still confusing to me about Christianity.

An acquaintance invited me to a Catholic church where American gospel singers were visiting. When I arrived, I spotted Mr Wells in the front row with the other clergy. Just the sight of him was enough to bring on a rush of insecurity, even fear. Suddenly, I was a child again, the trauma of my school days toying with my emotions. I tried to focus on the service.

The singers were very talented and shared their testimonies in between songs. I heard stories of drug and alcohol abuse being broken off by Jesus. One young man told us about his suicidal thoughts, which were completely abolished the moment he gave his heart to Jesus. His life completely changed, and he married the daughter of the family that had brought him to church. His story reminded me of Ecclesiastes, where everything Solomon did was vanity, wanting his life to end because it was meaningless. The humility, honesty, and passion in the man's story moved my heart.

14

Don't be fooled by me.
Don't be fooled by the face I wear.
For I wear a mask, I wear a thousand masks,
Masks that I'm afraid to take off.
And none of them are me.

Charles C. Finn

Growing up in a Hindu family and a strict convent school, my personality was conditioned to just obey and follow. There was no room to question or challenge any views. It was therefore very difficult to adapt when I finally reached the real world. I questioned everyone's intentions— were they there to help or manipulate? I read a book called *Games People Play* by Eric Berne[8] that helped me navigate these feelings and to feel more comfortable in my social interactions. The book talks about mind games and how people conceal their motivations in order to get what they want out of others.

While I was regularly attending church, I found weekly meetings in

---

[8]   Berne, Eric (1964) *Games People Play – The Basic Hand Book of Transactional Analysis.* New York: Ballantine Books.

the city where young professionals went to develop their social skills based on these findings. These meetings helped me interact with other people better. The principles from the book made me reexamine my past motives and actions towards other people. The introspection brought to light that I loved company because I was lonely. I wanted to make everyone happy because I needed their approval. I needed to be the centre of attention because I was afraid of being lost in the crowd. I was broken inside, but I was great at hiding it.

Going down this psychology path made me begin to question other people's motives, as well. As I furthered my studies on the subject, I discovered more about the many defence mechanisms that people use as a way of dealing with pain. As I read about each mechanism, a person I knew instantly came to mind that fit each description. I was left wondering, If we're not true to ourselves, how can we be true to others?

I remembered Jonathan Maraj's words. He had tried to explain to me that we lived in a fallen world, and it was in our nature to sin. At the time, I didn't want to believe that I was a sinner. But now I was beginning to understand the truth of it. There is a fine line between motivation and manipulation, and it was quite easy to disguise one as the other. I looked with interest at business psychologist Robert Cialdini's principles of persuasion: reciprocity, commitment/consistency, social proof/conformity, authority, liking, and scarcity.[9] According to Cialdini's theory, these six aspects contributed to the willingness of an individual to follow orders.

I knew from my cult studies that in the wrong hands, these tools could manipulate people *en masse* to do just about anything. This new way of thinking about their operations made me even more determined to dismantle cults and the damage they do to the naïve. Once again, I was in

---

[9]   Cialdini, R. B. (2007). *Influence: The Psychology of Persuasion*. New York: HarperBusiness (Original work published 1984).

my element, debating with speakers on their own turf. I was a good networker, so I had become rather popular in most religious groups in the city, getting invited to debate with so called gurus and fortune tellers. I must admit, I found a lot of pleasure in showing these people up. On one such occasion, a man recommended I read a book called *Why Am I Afraid to Tell You Who I Am?* by John Powell. I picked it up as soon as I could.

"If I expose my nakedness as a person to you, do not make me feel shame," Powell declares right at the outset, on page 10.[10] He explains that self-disclosure is really hard to accomplish because we fear being misunderstood or rejected if we open up to others. He says there are levels of close communication that people can achieve and encourages the reader to live at a constant level of feelings and emotions, the fourth level out of five total. This helps us to more openly and authentically communicate how we feel with others.

Reading the book, I found the greatest kindness—and really a great power, as well—is truth and to be true to oneself and others. The book also catalogues the roles people occupy that may be false versions of themselves. Roles like the clown, the conformist, or the flirt are easily slipped into because they feel safe. If we take on that persona, we don't have to reveal our true selves and we avoid vulnerability. I identified especially with the roles of the loner and the competitor, so it was interesting to read his take on them. Powell concludes that we need mature love to be in relationships, and the secret to good love is communication and giving over our true selves to the other person.

*   *   *

---

10   Powell, John Joseph (1975). *Why am I afraid to tell you who I am?: Insights on self-awareness, personal growth and interpersonal communication.* New York: Fontana.

I had been on my quest for truth for about six years at this point. I was learning every day and visiting new and old cults, all of them bent on converting me. I enjoyed debating more and more, always sure I had enough mental ammunition to carry myself through. I didn't care what their religion or belief was, I just wanted to prove my point. And despite my spiritual confusion, I kept going to church regularly. I loved hearing the testimonies, but I still did not have the patience to sit through the worship songs. I wanted intellectual stimulation, not music. The pastors knew who I was and often talked or prayed for me after the service. They were always friendly, so I permitted them to.

I was used to learning about Hinduism through fables, so whenever a preacher would tell a story, it stuck in my mind much more easily. I enjoyed those kinds of speakers and often approached them after the service to gain some clarity on their points. I also mentally graded their skills and learned from the really good ones.

In March of that year, the Hindu Festival of Colour, Holi, began. It goes on for two days and celebrates fertility and love. It is a time for people to get together and be full of joy, regardless of caste and ethnicity. Growing up, I went from being the typical child, excited to see and play with all the colours, to getting frustrated by how long the colours lasted, taking days to wash out. So I decided not to be part of the festivities this time and to stay home.

The music blared into my home, along with shrieks of laughter, and the smell of food floated in through the window. Admittedly, I was very bored. I was trying to think of somewhere to go where I wouldn't get bombarded with colour. Then I remembered a Global Mission event, a crusade that was going to be broadcast to thousands of locations in the world in 48 different languages. They were sharing the gospel to millions of

people all at once. I decided to go to the crusade.

I changed into an old pair of trousers and a shirt I didn't care for in case somebody splashed colour on me. Armed with an umbrella as a shield, I walked out of my home and ran to find a taxi to take me to church. As soon as I stepped onto the street, I was bombarded with balloons full of coloured water. My umbrella was useless and I could feel water dripping down my back. I ran as fast I could to the road, luck on my side as I hailed a cab almost instantly and jumped in.

It was an uncomfortable 20 minutes in the cab, my clothes dripping in water. By the time I got to church, it was noon, and I wasn't sure what to expect. The event had started at 9AM so I was already three hours late. I hadn't registered yet either and, as I stepped into the office in my subpar clothes, I felt very self-conscious. Even though I knew the pastor quite well, his elegant suit made me feel even more uncomfortable. I started explaining my appearance, but he just handed me registration forms, asked if I wanted lunch, and was relieved when I said no. As I filled out the forms, he explained that there were over 700 people in the hall, mostly pastors and Bible college students from all over the country. I told him I would be happy to just sit in the back corner and watch.

When the paperwork was done, I made my way to the back corner and watched the screen on stage that was showing snippets of interviews with people all over the world. They were talking about what it meant to be Christian.

"It is not taught, but caught." Said one African pastor. I liked the simplicity of that statement and was excited to see the rest. A Korean pastor named Billy Kim held up a can of Coca Cola on the stage. I was intrigued.

"Do you know that by the year 2000, the Coca Cola company has promised that everyone in the world will have tasted Coke. What about

Christians? Why can't we, who share the love of God, share the gospel with the whole world with such confidence?" This opening statement seemed both powerful and absurd. There was such a convincing call to action behind it, but I found it absurd that a preacher would use something like Coca Cola on international television to deliver a spiritual message. He went on to talk about God's love and the Christian mission to spread that love all over the world.

There was an intermission after his sermon, and when the lights came on, I noticed that everyone was dressed in their best clothes. I stood out like a sore thumb in my old shirt and trousers. It was the first time I felt out of place at church, with nowhere to hide from judging onlookers. The announcer instructed us to break into small groups for Bible study, and I cringed. I couldn't just sneak away and fade into the background. I saw a pastor gesture for me to join his group. I accepted my fate and joined, trying to make myself as small as possible so as not to draw attention to myself.

Everyone in that group had been there since the morning and had plenty of study notes. I was pleased to find that the group was discussing a few questions on love. They were exploring the world's view of love versus what the Bible teaches about love and how someone could reach others with the love of Christ. They were good questions, and I happily listened to the ideas that were jockeyed about, observing and not speaking. I looked around the group and locked eyes with a man who looked rather familiar. I realised I had seen that face at one of the cult meetings I attended. He was speaking very aggressively to the group. He clearly wanted to dominate the conversation.

It was irritating to watch and hear his condescending tone, as if he was the final authority on the matter. He was forcing his version of love on the group leader and suddenly turned his attention on me.

"Brother, you haven't said a single word this whole time. Would you like to add something?"

"I'm not Christian," I replied, "but even I know that what we're calling 'worldly love' is selfish at its core. 'Godly love' looks outward; it's 'love thy neighbor'; it's showing love of God by helping people—His people." The group fell silent, clearly not expecting the silent man in ugly clothes to say something like this. I felt so self-conscious. The cult leader, however, seemed more unnerved by my comment and attacked me personally, thinking I would be an easy target.

"Brother, you are not even Christian, so how can you even talk about Christian love?"

"I don't need to be Christian to know about the subject," I retorted. "You do not have the authority to define or hijack the conversation just because you claim to be Christian."

The tension in the group was rising, and I could sense the people anticipating a full blown argument. The leader intervened and asked if anyone else had anything else to add. The rest of the discussion lasted half an hour, and when we regrouped with the rest of the congregation, one person from our group was to go on stage and share some highlights and answer the lead pastor's questions. I could see each group representative nervously step on stage, not used to so many eyes on them. The crowd would laugh whenever someone was stuck on an answer. It was as though they found someone else's misery amusing.

When it was our group's turn, our leader asked for volunteers. I knew I didn't want the cult member to represent us, and I could see he was eager to be chosen.

"We should send someone who really knows what they're talking about," I chimed in quickly.

"If that's the case," the cult member mocked, his face red with frustration, "then why don't you go down since you know so much more than us. Let's see how you fare on the stage." I didn't like the idea at all. My ego was bruised, especially because of how I was dressed compared to everyone else. But before I knew it, I was walking trance-like towards the stage. I could see the cult member's face smirk in surprised excitement, waiting for me to make a fool of myself.

I could already here the crowd laughing. They saw how I was dressed, that I wasn't a preacher, and a lot of them knew I wasn't Christian. I wished the ground would open up and swallow me whole. My heart was beating so fast, I was sweating, and my legs trembled. The laughter rang in my ears. When I finally reached the stage, the pastor handed me a microphone, and a different kind of sound erupted in the auditorium. Now there was cheering, mostly from the Bible college students I was well acquainted with. The support was definitely encouraging.

"So what happened in your discussion?"

"We talked about the difference between worldly love and Christian love," I said. A bout of cheering rippled around the room.

"Go on, tell us about it," the pastor prompted. I could feel the crowd waiting to laugh at my expense. I didn't look remotely qualified for this moment, and they were sure I would fail.

"It is said that love makes the world go round," I began shakily. "It strikes across a crowded room, sweeps us from our feet, makes fools rush where angels fear to tread. Love has been portrayed as a force, a fuel, a drug, an elixir, a biological trick to ensure the survival of the species, a gift from God to remind man of his divine life." The room was silent. I began to feel in control again as their expectations of me were upended. The words flowed easily from my mouth.

"Love is a gift from God, to remind man of his divine life. When we look at the world we see that love is defined by certain feelings. Things like

I love tea, I love chocolate, I love football. But it is with the same feeling that we say, 'I love you' to someone who is precious to us.

"I have learned through my studies, and in discussion here today, the differences between eros, the romantic and sensual love; philia, the sense of affection or friendship; and agape, the divine love. This agape is the love Bible talks about. You must be able to love yourself and your neighbour before you are capable of loving God. If you can't love the person you see, how can you love Him you don't see?" I felt the curiosity in the room piquing.

"If you call yourself a Christian, then you are commanded to love everyone unconditionally. Love is not love if it does not serve or sacrifice, and that is the true meaning of Christian love. Remember agape love. You love your fellow man because you love God." There was no reaction from the crowd when I finished. The Pastor was getting ready to ask a question, and, once again, the crowd laughed expectantly, waiting for another opportunity to see my fall.

The pastor knew me quite well and knew that I wasn't a Christian. He settled the crowd with a sweep of his hand and continued.

"We Christians give so much to the world, but we are accused of not giving enough. So how much do you think a Christian should give?" The crowd was ecstatic. They assumed I was trapped and there was no way I could answer this question. I took a deep breath and, with a smile, began.

"Pastor, in the words of Mother Teresa," I said, "give, give, give, until it hurts. When you give until it hurts, then you can ask God for more grace and give even more."

"Amen, brother!" the pastor exclaimed. "Amen! May God bless you in abundance. Wow!" At this, the crowd came to a standing ovation. As I walked back to my seat, people reached out, shouting blessings and trying to shake my hand. Tears were running down my cheeks, an emotional release beyond my control. It felt like a dream, and I walked out and sat on the staircase, letting myself cry alone for a moment. I had never felt so fulfilled. Even in my simple clothes, God used me, raised me out of the lowest position to one of strength. That afternoon, I was rushed with admiration. People were thanking me for my words, asking for public speaking advice. Before this moment, I hadn't experienced such genuine admiration and the power of miracles.

My friends, however, continued to tell me that I was brainwashed. But when I told other preachers about this miracle, they told me I was touched by the Holy Spirit, and God's blessing was pouring all over me. And so, a new question had arisen. What did it mean to be touched by the Holy Spirit?

15

What the heart knows today the head will understand tomorrow.

James Stephens

Based on my investigations of the Christian faith, I knew that God the Father, Jesus, and the Holy Spirit were considered the Holy Trinity, three in one. They were distinctly different but were all God, fulfilling the monotheistic expectation. The only reason I grasped this concept rather quickly was because Hindus had a similar teaching. The one God, Brahman, had three different expressions; Brahma, Vishnu, and Shiva.

This and the constant Catholic intonation, "In the name of the Father, Son, and Holy Spirit" was all I knew about the Holy Spirit. Talking in depth with these educated preachers after I had just spoken on stage was a whole new and eye-opening experience. And while I didn't know what they were referring to when they said I was filled by the Holy Spirit, there was one thing I *did* know. I did not speak that way in my own strength.

Over the next couple of days, I turned the question over and over in my head. Who is the Holy Spirit? I brought my question to a former teacher, Mr Samuel, whose opinion I respected, and he managed to explain it in simple terms.

"The Holy Spirit is a person," he told me. "He is God, coexisting with the Father and Son. His purpose is to transform people to be more like Christ. To be filled with the Spirit means to have great joy in the Lord for that is your strength." I hadn't really heard many teachings on the Holy Spirit, so this was my first time trying to understand the depth of it.

"Can anyone be filled with the Holy Spirit? Anytime, anywhere?" I asked.

"Of course! Anyone can be filled, but they have to be obedient to God, be available and desire it. The Holy Spirit will only take control with consent. The Bible tells us, those drunk in wine and those drunk in the Spirit have one thing in common—they are being controlled. What differs is how the infilling of either substances or the Spirit changes their fruit. The fruits of the Spirit include gentleness, kindness, patience, and self-control. The other produces hate and anger. I hope I have, in some way, satisfied your curiosity, Sanjay. It's always a pleasure to see you," he concluded kindly.

Mr Samuel was never preachy, just conversational and always addressed my questions, no matter how absurd. Together, he and Mr Wells had moulded me into the person I am today. They were both God-loving and God-fearing men that built people up no matter who they were.

I started to wonder—was I really touched by the Holy Spirit? It was a similar feeling to the first Bible camp I went to, and I couldn't help but wonder if the Christians had used the power of words to brainwash me. I searched for answers in the Bible when my eyes fell on 1 Corinthians 2:1-5:

And so it was with me, brothers and sisters. When I came to you, I did not come with eloquence or human wisdom as I proclaimed to you the testimony about God. For I resolved to know nothing while I was with you except Jesus Christ and him crucified. I came to you in weakness with great fear and trembling. My message and my preaching were not with wise and persuasive words, but with a demonstration of the Spirit's power, so that your faith might not rest on human wisdom, but on God's power.

I was gobsmacked. The scripture came alive to me in light of my stage time. I knew that I would never have been able to perform the way I did on my own. I wasn't strong enough or wise enough. It was definitely a supernatural moment but whether that was the Holy Spirit, I was still skeptical. And how would I ever know for sure? No matter how much I learned, I still felt like I knew nothing. I just uncovered more layers of religion that I didn't know. But that didn't stop me on my quest for truth.

*   *   *

I went on a retreat where Jonathan Maraj was speaking, and as I pulled into the venue, I was excited to see him. He greeted me with a warm hug and told me there was a new guest speaker, Pastor Mathew. He had a Hindu background and was going to talk about God from this perspective. I couldn't wait. He began his talk by quoting some of the Hindu prayers that hinted at Christian similarities. Things about a Lord born of a virgin. Like me, Ps Mathew had stepped out of his Hindu bubble and set out on a quest to find the true God.

Hindus worship so many gods, so he wanted to find out which of these people he was actually crying out to when he was praying. He searched and searched until he stumbled across a part of the Vedas that actually acknowledged Jesus Christ. Many of the Vedic requirements were fulfilled by Jesus Christ in the Bible, for example, the need to have a saviour without blemish. Even the details surrounding his torture that were touched on in the Vedas were satisfied by the Bible. And *Moksha*, a Hindu concept of salvation, was fulfilled in the person of Christ. Ps Mathew had finally found the True God, and he accepted Jesus as Lord and Saviour.

I spoke to him after the service and told him I had never met anyone who linked the Jesus of the Bible to the saviour in the Vedas. It was incredible to learn that many of the verses in the Vedas related to something in the Bible.

My next retreat was in Orissa, East India, known for its plethora of Hindu temples. Here I met Pastor PC Hota. When I met him, his humble demeanour immediately reminded me of Jonathan Maraj. He, too, was born in a high class Hindu family and grew up praying in temples to multiple deities. On a visit to a temple as a child, a priest revealed to Hota that they kept the tradition of human sacrifice every April. He explained the practice in detail. Hota was horrified, and he turned from his Hindu faith. He disavowed the existence of any God.

When he moved to college, he was a brilliant student, and a Christian professor took a liking to him. She spoke to him about about Jesus. He wasn't very receptive, and he told her that if she ever brought up God again, their friendship was over.

But the professor was persistent and gave Hota a Gospel. He was furious and stormed out of the room. The teacher followed and simply said, "Hota, remember whenever you are in trouble, just try Jesus."

From that day, Hota avoided the teacher, sick of her preaching. He sat at the back of class, avoiding eye contact with her all lesson.

One day, the government issued a flood warning telling people to evacuate the area where Hota lived. He could hear people in his building shuffling to get out. But he was stuck in bed with a fever. He was on his own and unable to move. Hours later, after everyone had gone, the dam finally broke, and water started pouring into his room. In his fever-addled state, he decided to jump into the water and try to swim to safety.

Try Jesus.

He heard a faint voice somewhere near him. He looked around to see who it was but, of course, found no one.

Try Jesus.

He remembered the words of his teacher. He was desperate and had nothing else to try.

"Jesus," he sighed, "I don't know who you are, but if I live today, I will serve you for the rest of my life."

He jumped into the water and fell unconscious. When he came to, he was in a village 12 kilometres away from his hostel, where he'd been pulled from the water by the locals. He knew it was a miracle.

As the years went on, his Christian faith grew. When his parents found out how committed he was, they kicked him out and disowned him. He knew he wanted to serve the Lord full time instead of working for the family business, so he took a job in an orphanage. He joined a Bible college, studied to become a pastor, and started a ministry in Orissa.

The whole time he spoke, I was reminded of Jonathan Maraj. Ps Hota was so humble and gentle, but his words shook the whole auditorium, especially when he prayed. I spoke to him for hours after service to gain more insight into his family and how he felt about it all. He told me that it hurt the most when his parents refused to give their blessings when he got married. But as I spoke to him, I could see that beyond the pain, he was content with his decision. It hurt to leave his family but he was happily serving the Lord. It made me wonder how it was so clear to him that choosing his heavenly Father over his earthly one was the right thing to do.

*   *   *

Speakers often mentioned a heavenly Father, and I always tried to picture that image. My earthly father wasn't a great protector, provider, or teacher. He was just a man, ready to punish and beat me at a moment's notice, never protecting me from anything, really. And he hadn't ever been much of a provider, either. He was never there when I needed him. I can't ever remember feeling happy when my father was around. On the outside, people knew him as incredibly altruistic, helping others and getting praised for it. But behind closed doors, he was distant and cold.

As a result, when he had a long stay in hospital (more than three months) soon after I met Ps Hota, I didn't think much of it. Not only had my father been in and out of hospital for years, but I was accustomed to him using illness to emotionally manipulate the family. I could see my mother frantically trying anything to get him better. I did not have the will or heart to visit him, as my psychological wounds reopened whenever I was around him.

Weeks passed, and his situation continued to deteriorate, but still I refused to see him in the hospital. But my distance was clouded with guilt and worry. One day, a childhood friend, Chandy, a Christian, visited my father and he told me he donated blood while there.

"I am so fortunate to have a friend like you," I said as I hugged him tightly. "I am indebted to you. Thank you for your friendship and love."

"Sanjay, think about it," he responded. "If your friend on earth can love you so much, then imagine how much the Father in heaven can love you. He loved you so much that He died on the cross for you. You know more about the Bible and other religions than anyone I know, but your ego stops you from accepting the truth. You just have to surrender to Him and see what He is capable of."

The words struck me. There were tears in my eyes and remorse in my heart. All the people I had met that knew Jesus flashed in my mind like a movie reel. Jonathan Maraj, Kaushik, Ps Hota, Mr Samuel... Their testimonies flooded me, and the verse John 3:16 echoed above it all:

For God so loved the world that He gave His one and only Son, that whoever believes in him shall not perish but have eternal life.

For the first time in my life, I truly felt how much our heavenly Father loved us. It is the greatest act of love to die for our sins. I knew in my heart how much resentment and bitterness I held towards my own father. I was completely shaken and emotionally shattered.

"I know I didn't trust God," I said, "despite everything I have learned and seen. But I think I'm ready to take that step of faith. I want to surrender completely to God, and there will be no turning back for me. I am going to walk away from my worldly life and walk with God," I said eagerly. My friend was ecstatic. He led me in a prayer.

"Lord Jesus," I began, "I am a sinner, please forgive me for my sins as I forgive those who have sinned against me. Thank you for dying for my sins on that cross. I accept you as my Lord and Saviour." Immediately, I felt a burden lifted off my chest. All the remorse, bitterness, frustration, and anger toward my father melted away.

The next day, I went to see him. My mother was both surprised and thrilled. Before I went, I met with a friend who had connections to the best doctors in the city from his work with the Lions Club International. I requested help for my father.

When I finally made it to the hospital, my father looked like a completely different person. I was shocked and dismayed. There were tubes connected all over his body, and he looked shrunken and pale. I stood there in silence, staring at his helpless form. As I approached, he turned his head slowly and cautiously towards me, and I could see that simple actions took much effort. I sat on the bed beside him, and he tried to lift his hands to greet me. I took his hands with both of mine, but I was unable to speak.

"I am so happy you came to see me," he said weakly. "It was hurting me so much that you were not around. I know I was never a good father but I never stopped loving you. I am truly happy today."

Both of us were crying. I held his hands tighter.

"Father, nothing will happen to you. I have made arrangements for you to get the best treatment," I told him.

"Now that you are here, I know I'll be alright. Everything will be fine. You are a very capable son."

My heart exploded. I was crying uncontrollably. I didn't know what to do or say. I just felt like praying.

"Father, I am going to pray that nothing will happen to you, and God will heal you."

He smiled weakly, gesturing his approval, and I tried to pray. The only words I could muster were "God please forgive my father for his sins and accept him into Your kingdom. Please forgive me of my sins, too," over and over again, holding my father's hands tightly.

"Forgive me Father, please forgive me." It was as if I was asking forgiveness from both my earthly and heavenly father. I was reminded of *The Godfather*'s explanation of a man's need for two fathers to navigate a difficult world. I left the hospital that evening with both sadness and joy. I had finally reconciled with my dad. I had finally decided to accept God into my heart. I had my two fathers.

The next morning, I saw my uncle at the hospital with a sombre look on his face. He motioned for me to sit beside him.

"Sanjay, I need to tell you something, but you have to promise me you won't break down." I nodded in agreement, my stomach dropping. I knew something wasn't right.

"Just two hours ago," he continued, "your brother was talking to

150

your father, holding hands. And then… your father left us forever. Your brother is distraught and someone has taken him home. You are now in charge of all future decisions. I'm sorry this is so abrupt, but it's a delicate matter. So what would you like to do?" I had never been in a situation like this. I was speechless. *Your father left us forever.* I was stuck on those words, playing on repeat in my ears. *Your father left us forever.* I had only just found him!

But a voice inside my head started sounding louder. *Be strong and courageous. Do not be afraid… the Lord your God goes with you. He will never leave you nor forsake you.* It was a Bible verse, Deuteronomy 31:6, that I had read before but only now did the meaning really resonate with me. And it gave me strength.

My demeanour changed with this newfound resilience. My earthly father had gone to meet my heavenly father, and there was nothing to be afraid of. I was so full of courage, my composure shocked everyone around me. I took control and remained calm throughout the whole ordeal.

I organised the treatment and cremation of my father's body, making sure it was all done with dignity and respect. I decided to tell my mother personally about his death later so she had some rest before hearing the news. I was set on getting everything done quickly. I was most afraid for my mother. Hindu culture in India does not treat widows very well—although this has improved over the last few decades—and I knew my mother would be like an outcast, cursed and spreading bad luck. I saw widows begging too often to believe my own mum would easily escape the treatment. I decided I was never going to let any of that happen to my mother, no matter what.

I went home that night and lay next to my mother. I chose to save her the pain and a sleepless night until the morning, and she assumed father was still alive. I kept talking to her, trying to keep her spirit high. She always saw me as a child so it was easy for her to laugh with me. It worked to my advantage this time, and I was able to be with her until she slept. In the next room, I fell on my knees.

"God!" I entreated. "I cannot go through this alone. Not on my own strength, Lord please give me strength."

> *Because He lives, I can face tomorrow.*
> *Because He lives, All fear is gone.*
> *Because I know He holds the future,*
> *And life is worth the living just because He lives.*[11]

Lyrics from a song popped into my head. It was a supernatural thing, I was sure of it. A voice inside me kept drowning my doubt. *God lives. I am loved by a living God. I have nothing to fear.* I thanked God again and again. I was feeling strong again, in such a strangely amazing away. I felt peaceful, that everything would be alright.

The next day, at the hospital everything happened quickly. Relatives and friends were visiting, and I saw my mother enter. I wasn't ready for her yet. I didn't want her to see my father's dead body in such an undignified environment. I knew how it would affect her and would rather she saw it when it was prepared and treated. But I couldn't control this moment. My mother went hysterical. She howled and cried like I had never seen before. It was a moment I'll never forget.

The body was taken back to our home to allow people to pay their respects. For the most part, I was still calm. My older brother came over, carrying a mango drink and snacks. Apparently, the day my father died, he had asked my brother to bring them on his next visit. My brother had always been much closer to my father and loved doing things for him. He opened the mango juice and broke down, talking to the body as if our

---

11   Gaither, Gloria & Gaither, William J. (1971). Because He Lives. Gaither Copyright Management.

father was alive.

"Get up Father! Get up! I have your mango juice, sweets, and crisps. Please get up!"

The pleading continued, as if he was expecting my father to rise simply through sheer willpower. I couldn't stand to see it. I felt so helpless seeing my brother, who was always so strong, break down like this. He lost all control and had to be carried away.

"WHERE IS THE WOMAN?" A loud and intense scream broke through the crowd of mourners outside the house. "Where is the woman? We have to break her bangles, get rid of her jewellery and her good clothes. Her life is over, she has to live in penance."

I came out and saw the man who was the source of the commotion. I had never been so angry in life. No one speaks to or about my mother like that. I grabbed the sharp blade from a nearby coconut vendor and ran at him.

"If I hear any word about my mother," I said in fury, brandishing the knife, "or if anyone even thinks of touching her, I will chop you right now. My mother will live the way she always has. I am her son, and I will take care of her. This is my first and last warning."

My reputation was notorious enough that people took me at my word. Nobody mentioned my mother anymore. For the whole forty day mourning period, I remained in control. No one understood how I was so composed but I knew I had the strength of God still filling me and carrying me through each day. Because He lives, I can face tomorrow. Because He lives, all fear is gone.

It was the beginning of a new journey I never thought I would take.

Part Six

Acts

16

The things which are impossible with men are possible with God.

Luke 18:27

As time progressed, my mother did not get any better. She wasn't coping with the loss of her husband. She wasn't eating or sleeping properly, and her health was declining.

"Mom, please. Stop torturing yourself," I begged her. "I don't want to lose you now, too. I love you the most and don't want anything to happen to you."

She did begin to slow down and made an effort to get herself together. Nursing her back to health was a huge task, but by the grace of God, she recovered step by step. My mother was a walking contradiction. She challenged the stigma of the broken widow, and everywhere she went, people saw it. But in private, she struggled. I continued to guard her, making sure no one broke her down again. It was emotionally draining and tiring, but I had my church as an outlet, hearing from God in those meetings.

"God is the God of all grace," the preacher was saying one day. "He extends grace, His unmerited favour towards us in so many different ways! Every good and perfect gift is from above, from the Father." I felt as if he was talking directly to me.

I learned that we shouldn't be fooled by our gifts, saying we deserve them or made them happen for ourselves. The truth is, we all deserve hell because we have all sinned and fallen short of God's glory. But God is full of grace and chooses to bless us with good things and offer us eternal life. The preacher went on to talk about the need to recognise our own sin, confess, and repent.

As a young Hindu, I had understood sin as external to myself, something that I could simply opt out of. But the more I searched within myself, the more aware I was of my sinful nature.

"We need to be broken down over our sin, bowing down to confess to Christ and surrender," he said with conviction before conducting an altar call at the end of the service. My heart had been stirred as he spoke, and I knew now was the time for action. I walked straight to the front, bowed down, and confessed again that I was a sinner and asked for forgiveness. It took a lot of effort for me to get to that point. In the past, I would *never* answer to an altar call for fear of looking silly. But this time was different. I craved the chance to humble myself, and I was here to surrender everything to the Lord. If I'm honest with myself, I had always had a big ego, and this was a huge step for me.

*   *   *

My mother had a widowed friend named Savitri who had three young daughters. I liked her very much for her kindness, her loving and caring nature. When her husband was alive, the couple used to treat me like another child and shower me with love and food. After her husband's death, Savitri tried to run her food grain business with very little success. People who were supposed to pay her husband back never did, and local businesses threatened her. In spite of all this, Savitri kept fighting for her daughters, pushing through to provide for them. I always felt sorry for Aunt Savitri.

One day, she came to visit, and I was more than happy to see her. As I talked to her, I was filled with warmth at her smile and gentle voice. I loved hearing her call me "son". She asked how my mum and I were coping with father's death. She was well aware of how society treated widows. I told her how much God's strength and grace had helped me, and I spoke of my new spirituality. She hung on to every word, clearly interested.

"Is there anywhere I can know more about Jesus?" She asked, genuinely. I gave her a Hindi Bible, and I saw her face light up, as if this was the most precious thing she had ever received.

"Sanjay," she said as she was about to leave, "You are an honest and gifted person. I have always loved the way you care for others. I want you to know that I will pray that God gives you more gifts so that you can continue to touch and bless other people."

Three weeks later, she visited again. She told me that every time she read the Bible, she felt a real sense of peace. Even when she was having severe stomach pains, it all subsided when she started reading the Word. She was so thrilled by the results that she shared the Bible with her daughters too. The girls found the same peace and joy their mother had talked about, and they were so touched by the stories of God's love that the whole family went to church and gave their lives to Christ. Now, they were running a home group for similar people in the community.

I couldn't believe it. It had taken me seven years to take this wonderful leap of faith, and here was this fearless woman already running a ministry. I didn't know what to say.

"Son, you are chosen by God, and I have been praying that God will bless you with more gifts so you can bless more people." she said again. I was thrilled and humbled to be a part of her journey. Even her personality was different. She was always kind and loving, but now, there was a new glow about her. She was more self-assured than ever before, and I could sense a childlike excitement and joy I hadn't seen in her before. This was definitely the grace of God working in her life. How great God is and how powerful His grace and word! I was really seeing God's power in action. I knew I wanted to trust God with all my heart, soul, and mind. I was growing excited wondering how God would change me, too.

*   *   *

After I accepted Jesus, I faced more struggles and temptations than ever before. There were job opportunities from all kinds of people offering money. But these people did not fit with my principles, and I didn't know whether to accept. Of course money was very attractive, but I was afraid of going back to the beginning, my life changing back to what it had been, emptiness hiding behind a facade. What should I do next? What would God want me to do? How do I know if what I'm choosing is from God? I was already expectant for God to answer these questions soon like He had so often in the past.

Sure enough, at a Christian meeting, the speaker was talking about the "two natures" of humanity: our old selves before accepting Christ and the second, childish one of a new believer. If we do not feed and nurture the new "baby" believer, it will not thrive, and the old version of us will take over again. It is therefore important that we pray, worship, and meditate on the Word of God to feed ourselves and let the Holy Spirit guide and bless us with spiritual gifts. We needed to ask ourselves, "Is this choice going to bring me closer to God or further away from Him?"

I was shook. Once again, God had spoken to me. But as the path continued, it wasn't easy-going. In light of my newfound faith, I was becoming an object of ridicule in some circles. I was pinned as the crazy one, or the sellout, the traitor. Like I always did, I challenged anyone who came my way. But I continued walking with Jesus, and my spiritual gift of discernment grew. The hardest lesson to learn was humility. I had such a hard shell formed around me to protect the fragile little boy inside.

It didn't help that I was often called to debate with gurus and hypnotists because people knew that I was good at it. In fact, it was an easy ego boost. I was talking to a casino astrologist once who was trying to convince me of his authenticity. He gave the generic lines that could apply to anyone. Since I had read so much about psychology and human behaviour, I, in turn, figured out a lot of personal details about his life: his upbringing, his education level, marital life and more. I revealed my theories to him, and he immediately accused *me* of being a psychic and was shocked when I told him it was a simple matter of analytical observation. We talked for hours after that, and I told him that because of his conning and lying and denial of Christ, he was on a path to hell. By the end of our conversation, he was much more open to the idea of God. I felt good knowing I had helped someone onto the path, and I knew that the skills for this encounter were only in me because of the grace of God.

I continued to encounter incredible testimonies of the power of Christ. People spoke of being healed after a simple prayer. The result would be salvation for the individual and an ongoing dedication to God. I heard of ministries born from these moments and the great reach these people had in their worlds. It was so inspiring to hear them. I loved God and His grace. He had a plan and purpose for my life, I felt sure, and I was hopeful for all the spiritual gifts I kept hearing about.

17

The only wisdom is knowing you know nothing.

Socrates

God's law is meant to give direction, wisdom, and joy to humanity. These laws govern our spiritual status and control our destiny. Romans 13:10 says "Love does no harm to its neighbour. Therefore love is the fulfilment of the law." It's not about following a set of rules to constrict and control our lives. It's a liberating thing that enables us to love freely. There were four distinct spiritual principles that related to my Christian journey.

The first was the law of faith. We are called and saved by faith. We have no right to boast of our own things because nothing we did got us saved. We believe in God in faith, not knowing the whole answer but trusting and depending on Him anyway. It's a supernatural faith that manifests in the spiritual realm.

Second, sin and death versus spirit and life. Again, prohibition of sin is not God's attempt to control and limit us. It is a way of freeing us and letting us live completely in that freedom. Sin always brings death; it's what caused the world to enter its fallen and broken state. But Jesus came to bring life. He wants us to live free and of the Spirit where real life can begin. It's a struggle to not only know what is right, but to act upon that conviction. I am imperfect and need divine help because I know I could never stand before God and justify my actions. I need Jesus.

Third, the principle of sowing and reaping. I had a vague understanding of what this meant when I was introduced to karma in Hinduism. This idea is echoed in a number of different disciplines, and I came across many of them in my research—particularly in self-help books. The Bible shows how this principle works and that we need to understand it to be successful. If we plant seeds of despair and hurt, that is what we will reap. God instructs us to sow good seed for things that bring life and expand God's kingdom. So that is what we will reap.

The final principle is that of thinking. Proverbs 23:7 says: "As a man thinketh in his heart, so is he." Our thoughts heavily influence our lives; our decisions, words, and reactions are a reflection of what we are thinking. The Bible instructs us to meditate on things that are good, pure, and virtuous in Philippians 4:8. Ironically, I had already found this to be such a powerful tool in everyday life. My parents had taught me about the power of the mind from their Hindu perspective. It was the same: what we choose to focus on can bring joy or despair.

*   *   *

The first time I heard people speaking in tongues, it was eerie and spooky. It seemed like the whole church was chanting, screaming and speaking in a language that didn't sound like any earthly one I had heard. It seemed like a moment of mass hysteria surrounded me. I felt uneasy, and it took some time for me to understand it. I found out that according to the Bible, speaking in tongues was one of the gifts of the Spirit which is bestowed upon the believers for the purpose of building the body of Christ.

One late evening, I was spending time with Mr Samuel and decided to ask about my new area of research.

"Sir, how do you earn all the gifts mentioned in the Bible?"

"I have always been impressed by all your research," he replied thoughtfully, "but there's one thing you still haven't fully understood. Salvation is not earned through knowledge but through Christ. Everything in Christianity comes from or to the cross. To love by faith is to trust God implicitly."

"And how do I know that?" I asked hesitantly.

"First of all, remember our life on Earth is temporary, so never get attached. Worship Christ and be like Him. Love others and serve others with all your gifts."

"But Sir," I protested. "It is easier said than done. Life is so complicated; there is so much pain, suffering, and temptations all around. How does one deal with that?"

"God is real and unchanging no matter how you feel. Whatever situation you are in, just tell God how you feel, for God is good and loving and knows every detail of your life and has a plan for you. And He always keeps His promises. The other most important thing to remember is that we were created to become like Christ, and that is a long, slow and a hard process," he explained again with ease.

"Why does it take so long Sir?"

"Because we are afraid to face and accept the brutal truth about ourselves which is both painful and scary," he replied sympathetically. "We are very slow learners, and there is a lot to unlearn, and it takes a lot of time to develop new habits. One has to be patient and persistent, for we are put on Earth to make a contribution."

"But, sir, how would you simply explain what living by faith means?" I asked. At this, he took a deep breath before continuing.

"Faith means trusting in God instead of trying to reason through everything. It means trusting that his Word is the best guide for how to live. That sometimes means choosing to act righteously in difficulty when it would be easier to sin. But you must believe that God rewards those who surrender their faith to him."

It was so profound, I don't think anyone could have explained it better. The way he spoke made me want to build a faith that produced the fruits of the Spirit everywhere I walked. I sought out this level of faith actively, and still it surprised me.

In my prideful state, ultimately trusting God was difficult. My trust had always been based on my inner strength, and I had always managed just fine. It was terrifying to even think of trusting anyone or anything else. But I wanted to know God's will for my life. What did he want me to do? How could I serve Him? I didn't want to compromise anything so at the end of every church service, I would be on bended knee praying for direction.

I decided to apply once again to the army to fulfil my childhood dream. In the last stage of the process, they realised how dependent my mother was on me, and they told me that she needed me more than my country. I was upset, and I could hardly believe it. But it dawned on me that "Thy will be done" meant His will be done in all things, even if it went contrary to what I thought I wanted for myself.

After looking after my mother for a few months, it was time for a change. I opened up a teaching centre for effective communication in the heart of the city. It was rewarding and challenging, always exciting, with students from all walks of life. I loved that I made a difference in people's lives and helped them achieve their dreams. One day, I was invited to a Bible camp conducted by Ps Hota. I jumped at the opportunity because I wanted to spend more time with him. It was held in a rural area, and I was interested to see the ministry of its poor fisherman.

The camp was full of highly gifted people, from musicians to painters to teachers. The group discussions were incredibly thought-provoking, and I loved the fellowship. Ps Hota took us on a boat ride to visit the local fisherman.

"Have you ever swum in the sea?" One of the boys in the group asked.

"Oh. No I haven't."

"Then you have no idea what it feels like." He laughed, a hint of mocking in his voice. It felt insulting and demeaning, reminding me of high school when I was humiliated for my lack of eloquence. My pride was wounded, and I stared hard at this boy, sure that I could see a challenge in his eyes. And I heard a voice. *If your heavenly father owns the whole universe, surely you can jump and surely you will not die.*

I immediately stripped down and jumped into the water. I felt surprisingly comfortable in the sea, moving with ease in the water. That is until I heard Ps Hota.

"Come back! Turn around and come back!" He threw a rope into the water, beckoning for me to grab on. I instinctively obeyed and saw everyone's frantic faces when I got back on the boat. Ps Hota was terrified, holding his head in his hands.

"No more boat ride for this man. Once is enough for him."

I apologised to him later that day. I didn't know what came over me, and I told him about the voice I heard. He explained to me kindly that it was not wise to test God. The devil will tempt us to do silly things. Even Jesus was tempted by the devil so we must be wary not to yield.

That night, after much prayer and worship, I fell on my knees asking for forgiveness. I found I was crying uncontrollably, that feeling from my first Bible camp in Calcutta returning. Soon, people gathered around me, joining in the prayer—truly a moment of fellowship.

Later, as I drifted off to sleep, I felt a supernatural peace in my spirit. *I will never leave you nor forsake you. I will restore you, and I will rebuild you.* I knew God was with me. When I returned home, I realised the true meaning of faith did not mean jumping of my own accord to prove a point. It meant being directed by God and not *needing* to prove my strength. On the boat I had allowed my pride and ego to overwhelm my faith, leading me straight into a dangerous temptation. But in the quietude of prayer that evening, I could see clearly for the first time the absolute necessity of humility before God and His power. Once I learned this, spiritual doors opened in my life that I never thought possible.

God was healing my brokenness. I had always felt alone, riddled with bitterness, depression, and emptiness. Nothing I did could ever overcome the pain, so instead I had numbed it with the business and parties. What I wanted more than anything was true and complete wholeness, and I knew the only way to get that was through God. To overcome brokenness, we need to realise that there is a power far beyond the greatest that a man can possess. And only Jesus has that supreme power. This realisation was mending my broken heart.

One day at church, an evangelist was speaking. He was known for the miracles God worked through him and the prophecies he would issue. All throughout his ministry, he witnessed miracle after miracle. God was using him in mighty ways! He was an incredible speaker, mesmerising to watch, and the audience was hypnotised by his sermon. He spoke about how God would heal those who give and how all their financial crises would be washed away. I grew very wary very fast. He was saying we should pay for prayer, and it reminded me of the cult meetings I had attended.

I watched as people poured money into the offering, expecting healing and miracles. When the evangelist called people to come forward, they fell over after being prayed for. It was like a magic show, and I found it bizarre. I later found out that this was called being "slain in the Spirit". It designated a movement of the Holy Spirit on the person, which is so strong that the person falls down.

This was my first encounter with this phenomenon. Was it real? Or was it a demonic spirit parading as the Holy Spirit to fool people? I decided to investigate a little further. I found some passages in the Bible that looked like they legitimised the phenomenon. Matthew 17:6 read "And when the disciples heard it, they fell on their faces and were greatly afraid. But Jesus came and touched them and said, 'Arise, and do not be afraid.'" I read similar things in Acts and Ezekiel. Scattered throughout the Bible were examples of people falling under the power of Jesus or the Holy Spirit.

The next time the evangelist visited Calcutta, he was expelled after a disturbance erupted into a rally. The media had called him out as a fake miracle worker, the moments of healing localised to the hype of the conference or service. He was cheating people for their money, and I knew then why my faith had to be in Christ and not in people of Christ. The Christian faith was attacked by many after this incident, and I was called a fool for being part of that community. Was I? And if I was, was it such a bad thing?

18

For many are called, but few are chosen.

Matthew 22:14

I had often noticed humble Christians being treated like fools, underestimated and thought weak. I now found myself being treated the same. The reality of Christianity is that it is a spiritual truth that comes with an earthly price. We don't go to church, pay tithes, or be good to stay Christian. We do these things out of a desire and love for God as we are transformed into His image. But these acts and our subservience to God brings ridicule and scorn from nonbelievers.

The Holy Spirit resides within us, and our desires also conform to His. Living by faith requires action. We can't just sit around and guess what God would have us do. We should diligently search and study the Bible if we want to hear from Him, and prayer reveals His personal will for us. This level of faith was difficult for the world to understand. They saw it as a weakness, a stupid thing to live by. My pride unfortunately reared its head again, and I was afraid of looking foolish.

But a preacher once said that everyone is a fool for something. No matter how good a person tries to live, only the blood of Jesus Christ will wash away those sins. And the Bible says that sin is truly the foolish thing. This particular preacher put a lot of things into perspective for me. Unnecessary speaking and the inability to receive correction also makes fools of us. Basically anything that is self-serving and not Kingdom-serving is foolish.

Meekness is not weakness, simplicity is not stupidity, and humility is not timidity. The beauty of loving Christ is that our value lies in Him. I didn't need others to recognise the truth because I lived for God, not for them. I was developing a whole new outlook on life. I knew by now that living by faith was not going to be easy, but I was ready to make a fool of myself in the eyes of the world if it meant being true to God.

We never really know what life has planned for us. We can have all the plans in the world and truly do all we can to reach an objective, but there is a limit to our abilities. The supernatural can ultimately shape our lives and change our plans completely. It was a crisis that most believers, myself included, often came across. I was anxious to know what my next step was going to be and what God's will for me was. I asked God for some direction, and, eventually, he showed me, albeit in a mysterious way.

Through my friend Chandy, I met a man who was the area representative for Trinity College of London's music and speech examining board. He had taken an interest in me and wanted me to join the team. He wanted me the next area representative and tried to recruit me multiple times, I was excited at this offer. I was not afraid of losing my personal freedom here. I sat for a few speech and written examinations.

One of the examinations was for the Performer's Certificate in Effective Communication. It was quite challenging, but I passed. The examiner asked me what my weaknesses were, to which I replied that I was self-taught. He was surprised at this information.

"In over ten years of being an examiner, I have never come across someone like you," he said. "Everyone tries to hide their weaknesses, but you are the first one who has openly highlighted his own." He smiled, clearly amused. "You are good—very good—but you really have to learn proper English. I recommend you go to London and learn the language from the locals."

I was excited by the suggestion. I had never even considered moving to another country. Is this what God wanted me to do? Is that where my quest for excellence was taking me? I needed a sign, some kind of assurance that this was definitely what my next step was.

I met up with a good friend Piyush Bhartia and his friends for an evening out.

"Sanjay, you are honest and intelligent," a friend of his began, "I feel like your qualities would be appreciated more in a western country. It would be so good if you had the chance to go abroad and really tap into the best version of yourself."

It came from nowhere, and I didn't know how to react. I hadn't met with these guys expecting to get any direction about this decision. Piyush looked on eagerly.

"Look," he said, jumping into agreement. "We have a family trust, and I love promoting people who really have a heart for excellence. I would be willing to sponsor part of your trip to London if that's really something you want to do."

I couldn't believe it. This was actually happening. But I couldn't just show up in London with nothing to do. I needed to find something, some opportunity to chase after. I found it while reading a magazine in an office. There was an advertisement for a teacher's training course in London. I contacted them asking for details and prices, and before long, I could scarcely believe it, but I was getting ready to move to the UK. I told my mum about my plans, and she was worried that I would fall into a decadent lifestyle of sex, drugs, and alcohol while over there. She had no idea that I had already been tempted by these things many times over and was finished with my partying days. She eventually agreed, on the condition that I was to report regularly to my aunty and uncle who lived there.

In a whirlwind of applications and formalities, I was ready to go. I was planning to be there for five weeks—four to study and one to explore. I really didn't want to live with my aunt. I wanted the freedom to explore the city by myself.

I knew that The Salvation Army had hostel accommodation in London, so I went to their local office to enquire. I climbed the steps of the building and heard people singing worship songs. I was drawn to the sound and needed to see what was happening. I peeked through the doorway and saw a large group in a hall worshipping God. Before I could turn to leave, an usher came and directed me to a seat. She had such a warm smile and radiant personality. I followed her, taking a seat right by the entrance. But I wasn't there for the service. I was just waiting for an opportunity to sort out my accommodation.

The preacher talked about baptism by the Holy Spirit and fire, his American accent full of passion and volume. He explained that baptism in general represents cleansing of Christians and included both water baptisms and baptisms of the Spirit. He said that water cleanses outwards actions, making a public declaration that our speech and decisions were now cleansed and renewed by Christ. Baptism of the Holy Spirit is much more internal; it deals with our beliefs and mind, unifying us more and more with the Holy Spirit.

Then he gave an altar call for those who had never been baptised.

"The Holy Spirit will be speaking to your heart right now. Do not resist it!" he declared, boldly, "you are not here by accident but because God has a plan and purpose for you to be part of his kingdom. If that's you, make your way to the front."

I was still hesitant to respond to altar calls. I often felt self-conscious or pressured when I responded, so I usually refrained from participating. But this time was different. My heart told me to go forward, more strongly than it had ever instructed me before. I tried to resist the urge but I just couldn't. I walked to the front, and the preacher prayed for me. I was slain by the Holy Spirit for the first time. It felt like electricity jolted through my body, and I fell forwards, ushers waiting to catch me.

My heart was overflowing with emotion, and I could not stop crying. I felt burdens I didn't even know I had lift from my body. My heart was getting lighter by the second. I thanked God again and again for touching me so deeply. I prayed for His guidance and protection for my journey to London. I left the Salvation Army, having completely forgotten about the accommodation! I had to go the next day to sort it out.

Soon, everything was in order. The toughest part was leaving my mother alone. I knew how dependent she was on me, and I prayed for her every day. My friends vowed to be there for her, for which I am forever grateful. It was time for me to leave. I had never been on such a long journey before, and I was surrounded by friends and family to see me off. I was about to fulfil my dreams, and I was filled with gratitude. I didn't know how things would turn out in London as I said goodbye to the people in my world. It was now or never—I had to live by faith alone.

*　　*　　*

I arrived in London to find my aunt and uncle eagerly waiting for me. My aunt told me she was about to leave for India, so I would be mostly alone for some time. I politely assured her I would be okay and could take care of myself. On Sunday, I visited a Protestant church, curious to see what a London service looked like. The preacher was talking about how God can use anyone, if we allow him to do so. He talked about missionaries and how many miracles God did for and through them.

I really enjoyed the service, even though there weren't many people. It was definitely a different environment, but I was welcomed very warmly, and everyone who made eye contact with me smiled or nodded in acknowledgement. I met a few people after the service and was complimented on my English. When the pastor asked me how I came to be in London, I told him a bit about my spiritual journey. He was fascinated by the story and asked me into his office to talk more. I left the church that day very happy. I loved how polite the people were!

The next morning, my uncle dropped me off on Oxford Street in the morning and promised to pick me up in the afternoon. I felt a bit like a child again, but what could I do? I was ready for my classes. When I got to reception, there was a clerical error that meant I was accidentally enrolled in the advanced English course, which I had to attend until they fixed the paperwork. I didn't learn much from these lessons, but I did enjoy talking to students from all over the world.

I met a young woman from Turkey whose name meant "joyous rose". She knew what it felt like being alone in a new country and wanted to show me around London. I was touched by the gesture and agreed. She told me she was living with her sister and her husband, waiting for her dreams to come true. The next day, she asked if she could visit me at my aunt's place and try Indian food. I said yes before I could think, and that evening, when my uncle picked me up, I asked if I could bring her with me, and he happily obliged. They got along in the tube ride really well, as if they were long lost friends.

My aunt was shocked to see her when we arrived home but managed to make everyone comfortable. After my friend left, I was scolded for what I had done and was told to be careful of girls as long as I stayed in London. I was here to focus on my studies, that's all. I couldn't blame my aunt. She hadn't seen me grow up, and all she knew of me was what I was like as a child. It was as if that image was still in her mind. But it was another reason to find my own place quickly.

The teaching system in the UK was a whole new experience for me. It wasn't the strict, traditional style I was used to, but much less formal. Students came to class dressed however they wanted and were even allowed to have tea or coffee during the lesson! It was one of many culture shocks.

Two weeks drew to a close, and I still wasn't in the right course. I also had yet to go through the list of hostels from the Salvation Army. Time was flying past, and my aunt kept telling me that I had to find a safe place to live or I would have to go back to India with them.

I found a place near Bayswater that would be the most convenient for me. When I went in to enquire, the man in charge informed me that they were shutting down, so could not accommodate any new guests. He recommended I go to Whitechapel. My aunt was adamantly against this, saying that it wasn't safe there. I had two more days to find a safe place, or I was to go back with them. I went back to the Bayswater branch and spoke to the manager again. He was sympathetic but firmly replied that there was nothing he could do.

"But why don't you try two doors down?" he said. "There's an international house for students that might have some space." I thanked him for his advice and went to the International House two doors down. I rang the bell and entered the reception area. The receptionist gestured for me to wait. She had the same aura as the Sister principal from my primary school, and I was terrified. When she was free, I asked her about any vacancies and was met with a strong "No!"

I tried to explain my situation but she remained just as blunt. Her body language was cold, and I could tell she wasn't interested in anybody's problems. I went to sit in the waiting area, composing myself and thinking of a plan. I was frustrated and disheartened. The emotions bubbled over, propelling me back to the receptionist.

"Why? I have gone through so much to come here and now I can't even do the course I want properly. Why? Why do things like this always happen to me?"

The receptionist was taken aback. She had no idea what to say. My voice must have attracted attention because the warden came marching out to investigate. I told her I had taken a huge step of faith for God and nothing seemed to be working out. She seemed touched and asked how long I was planning to live here.

"With the way things are going, five weeks but could change to five months, depending on how the course goes." She then informed me that there was a group coming the next day but there was a chance they were going to cancel.

"If you want it, bring money for a two week deposit and one month rent in advance, get a British citizen as a reference, and be here at 9AM tomorrow and wait. If they cancel, the place is yours." There was finally a ray of hope, slight though it was. I called the pastor I had met from the Protestant church, asking if he would be my referee. He happily agreed and promised he would be praying for my situation.

I couldn't sleep that night, excited for what the verdict would be. I really needed a miracle, and I was praying and praying. *God, if you have brought me this far, surely You will provide for me. I trust You for the accommodation.*

I walked into the office the next day at 9AM, waiting. I was on edge, nervous about the outcome. If this didn't work out, I had no idea what I was going to do. Noon rolled around, and still no news. At 5PM one of the staff members gave me the good news. There was a room available for me. We processed the paperwork, and I rushed home to show my aunt. I finally had a place to stay and would be able to do my course. My aunt and uncle were relieved, as they were leaving for India the next day.

I moved into my room the next day. There was a dining room, pool room, study room, and student kitchen in the main building where the offices were located. I was going to be sharing a bedroom with someone who would arrive shortly. After I had settled, I looked through the different courses I could do, calling various colleges for more information. Most of their courses had already started, and the ones that hadn't cost thousands of pounds. I prayed and prayed, hoping to find the perfect one for me.

*   *   *

That Sunday morning, I found the Holy Trinity Brompton Church, which I had seen on TV in India where people were slain in the Holy Spirit and experienced miracles. It was a beautiful Victorian building, double glass doors opening into a mezzanine, stairs leading up to the main church area. The greeters met me warmly and handed me a service sheet. The church was quite full, but I managed to find a seat, admiring the building as I waited for the service to start.

The ceiling was salmon-pink, gilded beams over the chancel. The woodwork and walls were a brilliant white, a huge painting of Jesus teaching His disciples on the front wall. An intricate stained glass window hovered above the painting, letting in a beautiful kaleidoscope of colourful light. It was a beautiful mix of modern and classic.

The service started with worship as everyone rose to their feet, led by the band. The lyrics flashed across a screen in large, easy-to-read writing. A church leader stepped on stage as worship closed, encouraging us to greet someone around us that we didn't know. I met three people this way, which I found so interesting. The sermon was about the grace of God, but my mind wasn't completely absorbed. I was more focused on my surroundings and concern for my future here. Then I remembered I was at a church known for their miracles. I wondered what I might witness.

The preacher spoke about God-given hope. I'm hoping for a miracle right now, I thought desperately. I could barely pay attention to the sermon, I was so anxious. What if I didn't find the right course? How would I spend my time here? I couldn't imagine going back home empty handed. I didn't realise that the sermon was over until the altar call for people who needed prayer. I walked up to the front and knelt down to pray. I was desperate. A young man in his early twenties approached me.

"Would you like me to pray for you?" he asked. I nodded yes, and he prayed a very simple and gentle prayer. He asked God to touch me deeply and reveal His plan for me. The prayer went deep into my heart, and I thanked him for it when he finished.

"Brother, you are not here by accident," he said. "A lot of miracles will happen in your life here, and God is going to bless you with lots of gifts." It was such a direct answer of assurance, just what I needed to keep pushing on. I was set on making this church my home church while in London.

As I was walking out, I saw some of the ushers handing out leaflets for a course called Alpha. It was designed to teach people about the basic theology of Christianity. My hunger for knowledge was as strong as ever, and I thought it would be a good opportunity to learn more. I filled in a form and handed it in, ready to start the course the following Wednesday.

If only my college courses were so simple. I spent the next two days frantically calling everywhere, but I still couldn't find anything. I was getting more and more worried about my future here. I was out of options so I looked in a phone directory and found contact numbers for Lion's Club branches in London. I made a few calls and managed to get in contact with a secretary who invited me to a meeting that evening.

I arrived at a fancy hotel on Oxford Street and was welcomed with open arms. Everyone introduced themselves to me and made me feel at home. I was called on stage to give a short speech about my work with kids through the Calcutta branch of the Lion's Club. It was nice to be there, but there was no progress on the college front.

I continued making calls to colleges the next day, but to no avail. I decided that I would just do the Alpha course for now and learn as much as I could about the English language and culture just from being in the city.

*   *   *

The Alpha course comprised 15 sessions over ten weeks and covered basic topics about who Jesus is and the beliefs of Christianity. There were post-dinner talks from the head of Alpha, and we were split into small groups to discuss the meaning of life. Part of Alpha was a weekend away. I was excited to start the course and was greeted enthusiastically when I arrived.

"Hi!" said the first woman I met. "You are…?"

"Sanjay Gupta." I replied promptly.

"Sanjay, let's see," she looked down the long list of names and ticked one off, "Great! I know it feels strange on the first night but don't be nervous. In just a couple of weeks, this place will feel like home." I joined the crowd of people and saw most of them were eating dinner. I wasn't sure

how long it would take for me to feel at home but for now, it felt a little like a dream.

Soon, a man who introduced himself as Nicky Gumbel walked on stage and welcomed us. He told us he was an atheist for half his life and understood where a lot of us were coming from and how we thought. He spoke in a very straightforward manner, which I connected with immediately. Nicky continued to talk about the secular facts that supported the historical accuracy of the Bible. I was hooked.

It was as if Nicky knew exactly what the audience was thinking and was determined to pre-emptively answer their questions. The whole talk was incredibly educational, and Nicky was also entertaining, so I soaked in every word. He talked about how materialism can never really satisfy spiritual needs. It reminded me of the revelations I got from Ecclesiastes.

We broke into small groups, and I was led by a lady named Lindy who was from South Africa. There were 20 people in the group from all walks of life. I was really looking forward to this moment, as I loved group discussions.

I felt so alive, like I was back in the recovery group in the Calcutta Samaritans. I happily shared my views regarding the concept of suffering, who Jesus was, and any other topic that came about. My loud bluntness was so different to the soft, polite speech of the other group members, and it occurred to me—perhaps this is what the examiner wanted me to learn from London. I loved how respectful the people here were, not pressuring one another to speak and putting forward ideas lovingly. I thanked God for giving me this incredible opportunity.

At the end of the night, Lindy handed out pamphlets Nicky had written that addressed the topics from the small groups. We all lingered after the formal part of the course, and I met quite a few people. I left impressed by how much everyone accepted each other and how easily they

opened up to one another. I bid them goodbye, promising to return and complete the course.

*   *   *

But my faith was being tested. I still had no proper college course since the original one fell through. My future was hanging in the balance, but I was not ready to give up. I had no friends or connections to help me. I was in a new city full of new sensations. The weather was so different from what I was accustomed to. I was used to the warmth of India, but London was cold. The food was repulsive to me. I began to feel lonely and helpless again. Everything had worked out so well up until this point, and I wasn't ready for it to come to nothing. All the college courses I found were only available the next semester.

Before I knew it, Sunday rolled around again, and I was back at church. I could barely concentrate on anything in my stressed and confused state. The worship was powerful, and people were dancing along to the music, the joy evident in the glow of their faces. I wished I could join them, but I was too distracted. The preacher spoke about God's unique and specific calling for all of us that is always good and perfect, even if we are going through an impossible situation. I prayed during that service that God would reveal my calling to me that day.

I still felt uneasy when, at the end of the service, I again went to the altar and bowed down in prayer. I surrendered every part of me to God, desperate for Him to reveal to me why He had brought me to London. Again, someone approached me asking to pray for me. The prayers meant a lot to me at that point. On my way home, I realised I was entering the fourth week of my trip. Worst case scenario, I would fly back at the end of week five having accomplished nothing except exposure to a new culture.

In spite of an overall feeling of loneliness, my hostel was full of people from all over the world, and I was starting to make some friends there. It was normal to greet anyone sitting on the same dining table, even if you hadn't met before. I loved hearing other people's stories and thoughts and being exposed to so many different cultures. Many of them had religious convictions, primarily Christianity and Islam. Conversations on these philosophies sometimes lasted late after dinner. The boys would often play pool after this, and I was pleasantly reminded of my university days.

But my uncertain future continued to trouble me. Was I going back to India empty handed? I called out to God for a miracle, but still nothing happened. I made up my mind that I would simply fly back home.

*   *   *

I had time for one more Alpha session, and the topic was "Who is Jesus?" Nicky started with his personal testimony, telling us about how he came from a Jewish family that didn't really practice. He had no real faith and was atheist for a large part of his life until he eventually converted to Christianity. I related deeply to Nicky's testimony and was touched by his story.

He went on to explain Jesus throughout history, both biblically and from other sources. I liked Nicky's style of speaking, combining personal stories with the Bible and other secular sources. He explained how humans crave love and relationships, which he termed a "spiritual hunger". I loved his sermon. It was refreshing to see someone so well researched present this information to me. It would be nice to do the whole Alpha course and dive deeper into the word of God, I thought to myself. But I knew that reality had caught up to me. I had to go soon, so I may as well enjoy the night.

I broke back into my small group with Lindy, who opened the meeting asking about everyone's week. I was impressed by how well Lindy navigated the group. She skillfully encouraged the quieter people to participate and smoothly cut off the chattier ones to give others a chance to speak. We went on to talk about Nicky's sermon and the importance of finding God through relationships.

At the end of the meeting, Lindy asked if anybody needed prayer. I don't know what came over me. My pride usually interfered when it came to asking for help. But perhaps since it was my last day, I didn't feel as self-conscious, or maybe my pride was finally giving ground to humility. I asked her for prayers, and she asked her second in command, a charismatic man named Phonsie Kelly, to do the honours.

"Sanjay, what would you like me to pray for?"

I told him I was looking for a teacher's training course and wanted desperately for God to open that door for me.

"Heavenly Father, we thank and praise You for Sanjay and his life and for bringing him here to this church. Father I pray that You pour out Your blessings on him and please open the door that he has been searching for. We give You all praise and glory. In Jesus' name we pray Amen!"

He hugged me tightly after he finished and I thanked him for the prayer.

"Sanjay, do you know who I am?" he asked me.

"Honestly, sorry, but I don't." I replied, sheepishly.

"I own several colleges all over the world. The course you're looking for started yesterday. I'll give you the number of my secretary. Call her tomorrow and join the class. Don't worry about money, I'll take care of everything."

I was frozen in excited surprise. I didn't know what to say. I was overwhelmed. There were tears in my eyes, and I couldn't believe this was happening. God is so great. His love and grace are beyond words. This really was a miracle.

*   *   *

Since the course had already started, I could only be an observer and complete the full course properly the next semester for qualification. But at least I wouldn't be wasting my time and trip to London. I joined the course and learned the best teaching methods from world class instructors. I also came to understand what the examiner in India meant by suggesting I learn English from the natives.

As the weeks progressed, the Alpha sessions became a regular part of my routine, and I was building close friendships there as well. Nicky taught me about the benefits of keeping a prayer diary to keep track of just how many times God came through for His people. I started thinking about my own life and the events that had brought me to London, as well as the provision of my new courses, including this Alpha course. Everything had been a gift from God.

I was happy with how everything was going in my world except, as time progressed, my money was running out. I hadn't been planning on staying in London long, and the lifestyle was expensive. I had been living there for eight weeks with no source of income, and I was getting nervous. I was starting to lose sleep over it. If nothing came up soon, I was once again facing returning to India at short notice. Again, I had time for one more Alpha session and then it was goodbye to London.

I was sitting in the empty hall of the hostel television room, emotionally tormented by my situation. I did something very unlike me and just cried out into the space.

"Why, God? Why do You have to do this to me again? Why do You give me one thing and then torture me every step of the way? I am living by faith and trusting You for everything, so why do You do this to me? Give me equal footing, and I will show You what I am capable of. I left everything for You, and here I am. Look! Look! Look! You are the father of the universe, so what is a thousand pounds for You? If You really knew what I was going through then You would have provided. God I give up! Yes I will go back home, for it seems this is what You want. If You can hear me, then please show it to me today."

I cried like a child then, glad that no one else was in the room. All those feeling of agency and optimism that I had when I was first coming to London had vanished. I felt completely helpless and was late to the Alpha course that night. The group noticed nothing wrong with me. This time, Nicky spoke about spiritual warfare. It was an interesting topic, and I was able to focus. I was excited for small groups. When small groups began, Lindy asked me privately how I was doing. I told her honestly that I wasn't doing so well and that I wasn't really in any mood to talk about it.

"I was waiting for you this evening," she said. "Somebody left a letter for you in church reception. They asked me to give it to you." I was scared. I had no idea what it could be and was worried that I was in some sort of official trouble. I took the envelope from her and opened it to find a fifty pound note, a very generous amount of money. It was incredible. But then, I kept pulling out bills until I was holding one thousand pounds in cash. At the bottom, I found a note that read, "God honours those who honour Him. Use this money wisely for the glory of God." I felt like I was in a dream. I couldn't find the words to express my astonishment, so I just fell on my knees as the tears ran down my face. All my heart kept saying was, "How great thou art! How great thou art."

I remembered God's promises, "I will never leave you nor forsake you."

I knew that God wanted me to be obedient and just trust him completely. Later that night, after our session, I met up with members of the group at the pub. I asked them if they had left the money, but no one knew where it had come from. They hadn't even known about my need. There was a great excitement among them as they too had witnessed another miracle right in the midst of the Alpha course.

What an awesome God we serve. How great He is. His love is beyond comprehension. I couldn't sleep that night or do anything but keep praising and thanking God. I was filled with a renewed sense of dedication to my future.

*   *   *

Drinking was so heavily ingrained in British culture, and the rowdiness, violence, and promiscuity that came with it was unsettling. It was as if the Brits couldn't have fun on a night out without getting completely drunk. On Friday nights, I was used to seeing vomit all over the bathroom floors of the hostel and was introduced to a whole new level of drunk that I never witnessed before. I wondered how much of London's crime rate was due to binge drinking. And, more importantly, was there anything I could do to help?

I figured the excessive drinking was the students' way of coping with their environment and combating the stress, pressure, and loneliness that accompanied their studies. The cycle was predictable—and depressingly familiar to me who had seen so many friends succumb to drink and drugs. I often wondered why they continued to put themselves through it. They drank, made bad choices, ruined relationships, and woke up regretful the next morning. But while I definitely didn't condone or participate in such frivolity, I did find myself tagging along.

Friday nights in London usually meant a trip to the pub after work, ordering a few pints of ale to unwind. Often, what should have been a good social time devolved into something more toxic.

I met many young women who had left home to move to London and struggled to settle down. They came from all over the globe and were having a hard time adjusting to the new culture and way of life. They forced themselves to drink to fit in, even though they never drank before. A lot of them found it traumatic and were constantly hassled by boys trying to sleep with them in their inebriated state.

Sex was practically as common as a handshake in the hostel, even though there was a curfew at 10PM. Somehow people still managed to host parties outside in other places. I was once invited to a small get-together hosted in the flat of a young Swedish woman. I soon discovered that it was overrun by drinking games and spin the bottle. I knew I didn't want to be in that environment and was more than a little put off by the whole thing. I quickly found an excuse to leave. The next morning, I heard the usual stories of heartache and disappointments and was glad I didn't participate. But I began to realise that people just wanted someone to talk to, someone they could pour their hearts out to.

I once read an article in a Christian magazine by Rev Billy Graham, talking about how immorality is as big an epidemic in our churches as in the secular world at large. He gave some surprising statistics about how many regular churchgoers were having sex outside of marriage. Looking around at the hostel and the culture I now found myself in, I was less surprised. People didn't treat their bodies as temples. They abused them and gave them away much too easily.

One morning, I was having my quiet time and asked God for guidance. I had had this small revelation that I wasn't here in this exact spot and situation by accident, but by the grace of God. I reflected back on my life up to this moment. All the people that had been in my world, especially those who struggled with addictions have shaped me to be who I am. I realised that God let me go through those experiences for a reason. I was in a position to handle my friends' questions about life's struggles, pain, suffering, philosophy, psychology, and comparative religion.

It was time to put all my past experience to use. My heart hurt for the people around me who just wanted to be heard, and I was willing to be that person for them. Soon enough, my room became a place of refuge. People would come to me for help and guidance. It was a safe place to share their hearts. People usually came at the end of the day to vent and release their sorrows. They usually didn't even need me to say anything; simply having someone sincerely listen to them was enough. I met a lot of people this way, heard many stories, and shared a lot of heartache in the process. I cried with them and hurt with them, breaking alongside them as they endured some truly devastating experiences. I knew that if I didn't have God with me, I wouldn't survive, so I prayed every day, asking for wisdom and strength.

I built a lot of rapport with the people in my hostel, especially the women. I told them that if anyone pestered them, they could let me know, and I would have a talk with the other party. I just wanted to support them. I knew what it was like to be in a foreign place with no one around to count on. I had been bullied growing up, and it hurt me to see these people having to go through it, too. I was more than happy to allow God to use me in their lives in whatever way they needed.

The hostel began holding services at the every Sunday, and the occasional prayer meeting as well. I took any opportunity I could to invite people to these meetings, which caught the attention of both the management and the hostel's chaplain. They found out about my faith and what I was doing with the residents and gave me the opportunity to host a prayer meeting and be the guest speaker on a Sunday service. I was ecstatic and jumped at the opportunity. I had nerves, but they were a backdrop to the awe I felt that God would use someone like me. But I was beginning to understand it all over again. God and brought me to this hostel for a reason—to touch the lives of so many innocent people. I was beginning to notice a pattern amongst the people who came to speak to me—they all were worried about the same three things: career, companionship and confidence. With God guiding me, I was sure I could help.

Soon, people started coming to church with me on Sundays, and some even joined the next Alpha course.

*   *   *

Most of the overseas students had entered the UK with a dream. They had a specific goal in mind and moved countries to bring it to fruition. The problem was, a lot of the time, they were confused about what exactly the career would look like. Money was their driver, wanting careers that would make them rich or famous, wanted by everyone. I knew from experience that this was a normal and universal desire. But they wanted all of this immediately, instant gratification. The illusion was toxic, making them do silly things.

The young women I knew would throw themselves on anyone who was even passingly handsome and intelligent, competing with each other and wasting time, energy, and money. And of course, it led to heartbreak, which they would carry into their studies, ultimately affecting their career, too ashamed to tell their parents of what was going on in their world.

The young men, on the other hand—most a little bit younger than I was—were battling the same things, but from a different angle. Like the women, they drank, slept around, and partied and were always miserable.

The "it" boy of the hostel confided in me one night that he could never marry a girl he had slept with because they weren't special anymore. These girls were merely a passing phase, meaning nothing to him. In all of this, he was waiting for "The One". How he thought he could find "The One" in the midst of this lifestyle, I cannot fathom. It was same for most of the guys I spoke to. I would listen to their heartaches, delusions, and disappointments for hours on end, trying to guide them, to get them to put their studies first and let the rest fall into place. It was a challenge.

I had some really good and long discussions on comparative religion some of the Christian and Muslim students. One wonderful girl I met from Finland named Marjut was doing a course at Kensington Temple Church and had a deep fascination with spiritual warfare. I was impressed with her passion and integrity. I even started attending a Kensington Temple small group.

One evening, I was talking about my experience with cults and met a man named Stephen after my presentation. He said he was impressed with my talk and felt he had to compliment me. I was so honoured and encouraged to hear him say that. He told me he wanted to keep in touch, and we soon became friends.

He invited me to his house where I met his parents. His father was a vicar of a church in Ladbroke Grove. It was a very pleasant dinner, and Stephen's family treated me like one of their own. We had a great—if a somewhat intense—conversation about world politics, war, and religion. His father was quite interested in my views regarding third world countries, asking rather pointed questions about their involvement in building arms.

"What would *you* do if your neighbour threatened to hurt your family, take away everything you had and rape your daughter and wife?" I asked him bluntly. He was clearly startled, not expecting this kind of reasoning. But he understood the point I was making. Stephen and I grew closer and closer until I was basically part of his family.

*   *   *

I was meeting all sorts of people in class, in the hostel, in church, and in meetings. Interestingly, a lot of those people were researching various spiritual practices. Of course, I was also fascinated in the subject so I would have lengthy discussions with them, detailing my experiences. I continued visiting various sects and groups around me, including some that were using discomfiting mind control practices—cults again. But I also stumbled across a group that was dedicated to helping people get out of cults and restore them to a normal, healthy lifestyle. It was my first time hearing of this kind of group, and I felt that God was teaching and preparing me for something similar.

The more time I spent with people at church, the more I was struck by how prevalent loneliness was—and is. People were searching for connection and intimacy, going to bizarre lengths to get it, but seeming to misunderstand their own desires. I kept praying for God to give me guidance and to help people overcome such loneliness. Once again, God came through for me.

He had given me the gift of empathy, discernment, and encouragement, empowering me to, in turn, empower others. Now, I could see how He was sharpening my mind, showing me new things about different groups that would prepare me for my next role in His ministry. He had chosen me to prepare the ground in His people for seeds of faith to be sown.

*   *   *

Around this time, I was invited to a business conference where Terry Waite was the keynote speaker. He spoke about his time as a hostage for in Lebanon while acting as an envoy for the Church of England—a story of breathtaking bravery and devotion to God. He was utterly inspiring. After hearing him speak, I was determined to try to help people turn their loneliness what Terry had called creative solitude.

At the hostel, I spoke with management, and together we organized debates, socials, group walks to the cities, short plays and church programmes and charities. These were fun but wholesome activities that got people together. I felt like I was making a more meaningful difference to what was beginning to feel like a plague of loneliness amongst my friends and acquaintances. I could truly feel God working through me, and it was wonderful.

*   *   *

Five glorious months of learning had passed by, and my teaching course was coming to an end. I was ready to return home to India a new person. Even though I was only allowed to observe the classes, I had learned a lot. Phonsie, who had organized my education, had become like a godfather to me and told me that I should come back next semester to do the course properly and obtain the qualifications. He said that he wanted to open branches of his college in India and would love for me to come on board to organise and run it. He gave me the necessary documents in case I decided to come back and take the opportunity. He treated me so well. He would always say, "If you need anything, just let me know."

The fact is, although so much positivity had come to me through my time in London, I left it with a heavy heart. I had made so many friends from all over the world, and it hurt to leave them behind. A lot of people came to say goodbye to me, and I was so emotional. I was moved by the intensity of the moment. I told them that if God wanted me to come back, I definitely would.

*   *   *

I was home. Mum was thrilled to have me back but she had become frail and weak in my absence. I was shocked to see how much weight she had lost. My first priority was to restore her to health. Since returning from London, I got job offers from all over the city, but none of them felt like the right fit. But I was back with my old students from the slums every morning, excitedly sharing my wonderful experiences from overseas.

Gradually, my mother's health improved.

"You have always been a great son and you have served me well," she said to me one day. "But I want you to achieve more in life. That will truly make me happy and proud. Why don't you go and finish the course you intended to do? The doors are opened, and I don't want you to miss this opportunity."

"But I don't want to leave you alone, Mother," I replied.

We had the same discussion over and over for almost nine months until she finally persuaded me to take the steps. After plenty of deliberation, I booked the tickets back to London and my accommodation in the hostel two weeks before semester began. The flights were cheap, and I had saved enough money for any expenses I might need. Before I could finalise the payment, however, something completely unexpected happened. Princess Diana died suddenly, and there was a huge demand for plane tickets to London. The price skyrocketed, increasing by £300, which would consume most of my savings. There wouldn't be enough left to live on.

In the moment, I thought this might be a sign that I should not go to

London. I prayed and prayed. I didn't know what to do, but if God wanted me in London, He was going to have to provide the extra £300. I left the prayer at that, already partially convinced that it was God's will that I stay in Calcutta and take care of my mother. But God is an awesome God and a miracle worker.

At around 10AM the next day, there was a knock on the door. I opened it to find a postman handing me a registered letter from London. I signed for it and opened it anxiously, with the same trepidation I felt when I opened the anonymous letter at Holy Trinity. I pulled out the paper and was amazed. It was a cheque for £300 from someone I had met at Holy Trinity. There was a note:

> *Dear Sanjay, it was very good to meet and pray for you recently at Holy Trinity and at St Paul's. I felt that the Lord wants us to give you this with and for His blessing. Keep being radical for Him and stay centred on the only true Rock!*
>
> *Best Wishes, William and Ali Briston*

I was in tears, lost for words. God had come through again. He never forgot me, not once, and He knew exactly what I needed. But I still needed clearance from the Foreign Exchange Department of the government. Any money that came to the country had to be cleared by the Indian government, and I had to prove why and from where the money was sent.

I told the officials that God had spoken to these people and told them to send me the money, and, of course, they thought I was bluffing. I showed them the note and stamped envelope. I shared my testimony up the chain of officials, and some were astonished, others thought I lost my mind. They wanted a bribe in exchange for clearing the cheque. And yet, the mere idea that the money might be from God made them wary and fearful. In the end, it was cleared without any bribes.

My faith in God was at an all-time high. I was experiencing His power in action over and over again. I noticed, however, that His miracles would always happen at the last possible moment, letting me build up fear and trepidation. I felt like God was teaching me to trust Him completely and not to rely on my own strength.

Soon enough, all the preparations were complete and I was ready to return to London.

Part Seven

Revelation

19

We become the stories we tell ourselves.

Michael Cunningham

It was wonderful to be back in London. There were both old and new faces at the hostel, and it felt great to be with friends again. But the sudden demise of Princess Diana cast a shadow over everyone and everything. Heartbreak was thick in the air.

The hostel was across from Kensington Palace and Hyde Park, and we saw thousands of people offering their condolences on a daily basis. The queue for the official condolence register was always very long and full. But I queued with hundreds of others waiting to get into the Palace to pay my respects. There were speeches from dignitaries from all over their world. It was a strange atmosphere.

Her funeral naturally attracted plenty of attention, even after a week of worldwide mourning. In light of this tragedy, people were beginning to publicly ask big questions again: What is the meaning of life? If there is a God, then why did He allow this?

Every morning, after my morning prayer and quiet time, I tuned into the Christian radio station and listened to various preachers. One of the most popular subjects on these radio shows was the desire for relationship and intimacy. The radio station preacher observed that the three most prominent questions were: Who is the right person? Where do I find them? And how do I know if it is love?

One of my favourites, American pastor Chip Ingram, beautifully explained how to discern the difference between love and infatuation. God, he explained, wants us to become the right person through our faith in Him, and only then can a relationship with someone else flourish. He also talked about eros, philia, and agape, the three different types of love. I knew about these words before, but Chip communicated their meanings so well that they each had new meaning to me. He talked about sexual purity and intentionality.

I bought all his tapes on the subject and others as well. The more I listened to them, the more I was able to solidify my own reasoning, until I felt equipped to tackle the promiscuity that was so prevalent in the hostel. Armed with this knowledge I set out to slay the dragon of doubt and confusion around me. This was the start of a time when God used me in a mighty way through discussions, debates and, later, seminars and lectures. And then one day, I was the one on the radio.

*   *   *

Soon after my return, my dear friend Stephen got in touch with an offer for me to join his new creative marketing company. He needed help building the business, and he wanted me to bring my boldness, confidence and communication skills. I worked part-time for over a year with him, handling a social and political issues for a Christian issues. I even had the opportunity to go to Parliament regularly, where I procured materials for the magazine and met politicians.

My skills helped the company to make inroads into unchartered territories, including the London Chamber of Commerce. I attended many networking events on the business's behalf, and got to know some powerful people during this work.

The first time I went to the London Chamber of Commerce, it was a grand evening pre-Christmas party. Music, drinks, and conversations were flowing all around. I stood alone in a corner and observing and absorbing the proceedings when suddenly I heard a husky voice from the side, "Hi! Is this your first time here?" I truthfully nodded and replied, "Yes."

He asked in an authoritative voice, "So, tell me about your organization."

I replied, "Why don't you go first?"

He told me all about his powerful firm, how they had offices in 133 countries around the world. They did all sorts of deals from building bridges to promoting and buying and selling companies. When he finished bragging, he asked me, "What about you?"

Without a moment's hesitation, I said with a smile, "My father owns the whole Universe."

He was completely taken aback. He never expected such a reply. Then gathering himself together he said, "Do you know how rich I am?" I wondered where this was going.

"I am so rich," he went on, "that I have properties in every part of the world, and last month I bought my wife a mansion in Scotland for her birthday. I have three secretaries and it takes at least six months to get an appointment to see me. But you know what—I do not have the confidence to speak the way you do. What do you have that I don't have? I really want to know more about you?"

I told him it was my faith in God that gave me the power, courage, and confidence. He asked me if I would have lunch with him.

We did meet for lunch and I shared my testimony with him. He found Stephen's company too small for his kind of business, but he asked me to jump ship and join him at his own company. I politely declined and told him I had other plans. He asked me to get in touch with his secretary if I ever changed my mind.

*   *   *

At the hostel, there was never a dull moment, especially during meal times. I met a guy from America named Vincent. He was around 25 with a long beard and long hair. He was into the New Age movement, and he came to London to attend the Mind Body Spirit Festival. He was particularly interested in the sessions on yoga, meditation techniques, mind control, and healing through right thinking.

"God is energy," he told me. "All the energy in the universe—it's all God, so God is in everything. If we can just make ourselves aware of it, if we can see it, we can find our reality. Imagine what we could do, what humanity could do, if we could all focus on that energy instead of all this physical stuff."

It all sounded very familiar from my time exploring cults. He explained that he had been delving into occult practices like channeling spirit guides, contacting extraterrestrials, and consulting psychics. He believed in manipulating the flow of divine energy through therapeutic touch, yoga, and martial arts, and using Feng Shui to improve the energy balance of a room.

His passion was infectious, and I was really enjoying the conversation. I knew from experience that this kind of movement is not an organised religion. It is simply a worldview that has blended together the spirituality of Eastern religions. I tested his knowledge and understanding on these subjects, asking him many questions.

"What kind of meditation do you practice?" I asked. He was dumbfounded. He did not know what to say, unaware perhaps that "meditation" wasn't just one concept. I tried again.

"Which type of yoga do you practice?" Still, silence.

"Okay… what philosophy do you practice?"

At this, he brightened up and gave a rather strange answer.

"Well, it's a bit of Greek, a bit of Indian, and a bit of Oriental."

In the end, he admitted that he was still learning. I left the conversation there, knowing from experience that people who are all over their place in their thinking are actually nowhere in particular.

I was keen, however, to visit the Mind Body Spirit Festival, and the opportunity presented itself. Marjut invited me to go with her. She was going to be working the Kensington Temple Church stall at the festival, to try to reach out to people through prayer. She contacted me, enthusiastically asking me to join the team so I could interact with other members of the New Age movement. Mystical symbols like pyramids and the all-seeing eye were scattered across festival photos like confetti. The whole purpose of the festival, I was told, was to offer the very best in life-changing experiences of healing, personal growth, and transformation.

20

Do what thou wilt shall be the whole of the Law.

Aleister Crowley

I spent the next few days completely absorbed in researching the festival. I was reminded of a pastor I once heard speak about New Age concepts. He talked about how things like mystical humanism and the human potential movement were gaining traction and becoming more popular in mainstream society. Buzzwords like "awakening," enlightenment," and "self-actualisation" were abundant in the festival literature, promising unity and positive change. He'd said that there were 80,000 registered witches, wizards, and new age practitioners in London alone!

I knew the Bible had explicit instructions to abstain from such activities. Over the years, I've heard many sermons and speeches about the occult lifestyle, and I understand the appeal. It's dark and mysterious, and it gives the illusion of control over our own lives. But it becomes addictive and destructive. Yet, many Christians fall into these occult practices, enticed by the promise of instant gratification, communicating with deceased loved ones and fortune telling. Even "innocent" witchcraft—magic that claims to work for the peace and unity of the world—is condemned in the Bible. It's very clear: God is the only way to salvation and is the author of peace. No amount of human magic or wizardry can possibly outshine Him.

I have seen and experienced the power of evil and know how subtly it enters people's lives, often behind the façade of abstract spirituality. Amidst all of this spiritual warfare, I had been blessed to discover the power of Jesus, and now I held firm to my faith. Many of those at the festival were in fact seeking this kind of deliverance, hoping for a quick fix. But deliverance is a process, not the work of a moment.

* * *

Finally, the day came, and I was excited to be at the Mind Body Spirit Festival. I knew I would encounter fake spirituality. My grandfather related the idea of spirituality to Hindu teachings of *adhyatma*, a kind of personal truth. My moral science classes in convent school gave a very Christian definition of spirituality as the moral virtue by which we render to God the worship and service He deserves. Between these two, I grew up essentially understanding spirituality as religious practices of piety towards God as the creator of the universe, whoever that might be. But New Age believers rejected religious dogmas and rules in exchange for their personal freedom, what is sometimes termed "spiritual humanism". The festival was advertised as "an exhibition covering the spiritual, psychic and paranormal featuring mystic arts which transcend ordinary human knowledge."

I entered the hall and was immediately greeted by a lineup of witches, wizards, tarot card readers, palmists, life coaches—you name it. It was packed. Hundreds of stands, workshops, and demonstrations filled the place. I came across a demonstration that was teaching people how to connect with their spirit guide and guardian angels. They also taught the practical use of crystals to develop psychic awareness. And of course, the appropriate products were being sold to everyone there.

I came across a number of stalls that charged between £20 and £40 to answer questions about health, prosperity, and relationships. As soon as they saw me looking at their stall, one of them jumped at me, ready to explain their services. I wanted to know where they got the spirits from, and one replied, "We get them from the higher world."

"As far as I know," I replied, "the only place these spirits can be found is with the devil, and just out of curiosity how much commission do you pay them?" This infuriated this man considerably.

"Are you a born-again Christian?" He asked, angrily.

I told him bluntly that I was, and his face became red with anger, demanding I should leave at once. I was used to this kind of reaction. Most of the time when I talked about any other belief system, people would have no objections, but the moment I would mention the name of Jesus, people went ballistic. It was like a visceral reaction; they didn't like it. It convinced me very early in my search that the name of Jesus had power.

I moved on, continuing to browse the stalls, surprised to find a CD with pictures of Hindu gods and goddesses. It claimed authenticity with chakra images on the other side. I could see how they were trying to capture the naive and vulnerable with persuasive presentations. Then I came across something called an aura picturing machine. I found this stall, curious about what exactly it offered. The people who ran the stall told me it was about "having a visual reference of the body's metaphysical state" to enhance healing. They claimed it was extremely beneficial, visually validating auras and chakra changes for those who are unable to see energy channels. The whole time they were speaking to me, I was thinking about how interesting a method this was to con people and make money.

I carried on, finding rows and rows of spiritual gurus. There were many eastern mystical groups peddling different kinds of yoga, meditation, and lessons involving consciousness, laws of karma, and self-realisation. I even came across a section dedicated to Deepak Chopra.

The most common theme I found at this festival was that there was no need for redemption, salvation, or sanctification in New Age philosophy. When I spoke to New Age followers about Jesus being God, they simply shrugged it off, insisting that Jesus was no more a god than any one of us.

Marjut and her friends, meanwhile, were offering prayers of appeal in the Kensington Temple stand. There were a few takers, and I was told that some of them were surprised that they were not charging anything for their services. To me, that spoke volumes about the mentality of the festival. People were viewing spirituality through a commercial lens, a mere commodity that can be traded and sold. At the end of the day, I reflected on what had transpired at the festival and all the cults I had encountered. A poem came to mind.

Our New Religion
First dentistry was painless.
Then bicycles were chainless,
Carriages were horseless,
And many laws enforceless.

Next cookery was fireless,
Telegraphy was wireless,
Cigars were nicotineless,
And coffee caffeineless.

Soon oranges were seedless,
The putting green was weedless,
The college boy was hatless,
The proper diet fatless.

New motor roads are dustless,
The latest steel is rustless,
Our tennis courts are sodless,
Our new religion—godless. [12]

*   *   *

I came across a few people claimed god was speaking to everyone all the time, if only we would listen. And that everything including people are god. This concept was very popular when I was growing up. To me, it bore an unnerving resemblance to Genesis 3:5 which details one of Satan's original lies: "You will be as God"

More disturbingly people were peddling a kind of relative morality, where there was no right or wrong way to live, and death was merely an illusion. I found these new age philosophers to be as spiritual salesmen, justifying selling their con by naming it a revelation from God

*   *   *

I soon signed up to another Alpha course, the follow-up to the first round, at Holy Trinity Brompton. It was led by Dr Jonathan Tan, a dental

---

[12]   Guiterman, Arthur (1936) *Gaily the Troubadour*. Boston: E.P. Dutton.

surgeon. I was impressed with his passion for the Word of God and his desire to serve the community. There was something about him that calmed everyone down. He was a great conversationalist and a great listener.

This group was smaller than the last Alpha course. As time went by, we became very close, and when we were nearing the end of the course, he told us we had an opportunity to join a Holy Trinity home group. I was delighted to hear that he was running one at his house in Sloane Square and everyone was welcome. A lot of us decided to join.

We would meet at his house every fortnight, for dinner, worship, and Bible study. Jonathan would always provide a home cooked meal for us, despite his busy work schedule. I marveled at his generosity and humility. I loved his home group. It was such a wonderful place for fellowship and to build support for one another, focusing on serving those outside the group.

I knew that home groups were actually how the early church originally met. In the Bible the word for church, the Greek *ekklesia*, did not denote a building, but a gathering—of Christians. I felt strongly that this is how we should view church. Despite how beautiful and awe-inspiring many church buildings are, it was the gathering of Christians in God's name that held the meaning of church. And this home group encompassed all of that.

Jonathan's home group provided physical and spiritual food. The personal testimonies from my fellow group members and Jonathan touched my heart every time I was there. I was surprised to learn that Jonathan had not always been a believer. He had been touched by the Holy Spirit who transformed him completely. Jonathan always prepared great messages to share, and one of his most powerful ones that moved me was about blessings and curses.

I had heard other speakers discuss this subject, but not the way Jonathan did. He explained that the Bible teaches the importance of expressing gratitude to God for everything He has given to us. Moses taught the Israelites about tithing, the principle of giving 10% of their income to the Levite, stranger, orphan or widow. And when tithing is done with a generous spirit and grateful heart, it will bring in blessings from God.

I learned the importance of obeying God and controlling the tongue. Jonathan talked about different kinds of curses including biblical, witchcraft, self-imposed, and generational. He taught us that curses could be broken through repenting of our sins and the sins of our family, across generations. All curses can be broken in the name of Jesus, and we can be covered with the protective blood of Jesus. Above all, he said, we must be faithful in this, seeking forgiveness and repenting daily, and finding support in each other.

Jonathan then asked each of us what curses might be affecting us. He then prayed for each group member. When he reached me, I said I felt like my financial life was cursed, inherited from my ancestors who worshipped money. Along with Kali, we used to pray to the goddess of wealth, Lakshmi, every morning and evening. Jonathan prayed a simple, yet powerful prayer asking God to break every generational tie and financial curse that I had inherited from my family and set me free. I felt my whole being shaking with his prayer, and I was awash with relief.

Jonathan then showed me how to tithe 10% to the church. From that day onwards, I followed God's word, and I have never had financial trouble again. No matter how much I earned, I always gave 10% of my income to the church. God has always provided in abundance for my needs. I was amazed and inspired to study the subject more deeply.

21

God is like the sun; you cannot always look at it, but without it, you cannot look at anything else.

G.K Chesterton

Our home group, along with others in the area, joined a new pastorate run by a man named David Hurst and his wife Deirdre. I instantly noticed the way that anyone who had nowhere else to go was welcomed. It was a warm, friendly, and extremely welcoming place. I was amazed when, during the offering, David announced, "Whoever wishes to give is most welcome to do so, and whoever needs money, is most welcome to take what they need." I had never seen a place where people were encouraged to take just as much as people were encouraged to give.

One Friday evening, I was sitting in the dining hall, ready to have dinner. Each table was set up to accommodate up to 20 people, but I was mostly alone.

"Is this chair empty?" I heard a sweet and gentle voice ask.

I looked up and saw a beautiful young woman, with long blond hair with the most amazing smile. She was holding her dinner plate, pointing to the empty chair across from me.

"Yes! Sure!" I began to stutter. "By all means, please sit down." She put her plate across from me and went back to fetch cutlery and a glass of water. She settled back down in her seat and looked at me.

"Hello! How are you?" I confess that I was surprised by her direct approach.

"I'm fine thank you. How are you doing?" I replied politely. We continued talking, and I was pleasantly surprised to find that she was actually really interested in what I had to say and listened attentively. She had an air of elegance about her. Her hand movements, smile, and accent told me she came from a cultured and posh background. After I told her how busy my day was, she said the most touching thing.

"So you care for everyone... who takes care of you?"

"What makes you say that?" I asked, trying to hide how surprised I was.

"People here, especially the young ones, talk about you.," she said matter-of-fact. "They say that you are a very caring person and always there to help anyone in need. I would love to do what you do—the way you touch their lives." I was so moved by these words.

"I was taught from a very young age that we all have a moral obligation towards society," I replied. Mr Wells' words came to me. "If you are not part of the problem then you should be part of the solution. I trust God and He takes care of me."

"Wow!" She exclaimed. "What a great value to teach a child."

"So I'm Sanjay," I said with a smile. I wanted to know more about her. "And you are...?"

"Oh! I'm Sophia!"

"It's a pleasure to meet you. Where are you from?"

"Athens, Greece."

Before I knew it, I was completely immersed in conversation about Greek philosophy, even some of the tragedies I knew from my school days. She was very clever, correcting me on the pronunciation of ancient Greek words.

We talked for ages, covering so many different topics. When we touched on the subject of marriage and divorce, I could see that I had touched a nerve. She looked at me sadly and spoke in a soft voice.

"Why can't people live happily together after they get married?"

"Because people don't know the difference between love and infatuation," I replied tentatively. The conversation veered into pretty deep waters. We talked about how society is so particular about what makes a person "perfect" as a partner that it creates an unachievable standard. Inevitably everyone ends up disappointed.

"Most people don't really understand investment," I said. "Psychologists say that if you "fall in love," you're surrendering your own self to that person. And when you fall out of love, you get yourself back. But if you *invest* in a relationship, you work together to cultivate something between you that grows."

"So then, tell me your definition of love?" She asked abruptly. It was unexpected and required more than reciting or quoting a textbook. I pondered for a moment before answering.

"The first definition of love I learned was from my mother—it is a self-sacrificial act. To love someone means to nurture, nourish and to give freely, even if it costs you a lot." Then I said that the greatest love story ever told is the Bible. I quoted John 3:16, "'God so loved the world that He gave His only begotten Son that whoever believed in Him should not perish but have an everlasting life.' It is the greatest sacrifice anyone can give. The Bible gives the true explanation of love."

We continued talking about the different types of love in the Bible. I explained to her that I was born again Christian, that I lived by faith and trusted God for everything. I even told her a little about my journey and the miracles I experienced at Holy Trinity.

"Wow... you can write a book, you know?" She told me. We laughed about it.

Then I glanced at my watch and realised it was already 9PM! We were so engrossed in our conversation that we didn't realise it had been four hours and we were the only two left in the dining hall.

Despite how late it was, we continued talking long into the night. We talked about society's expectations about sex, the idea of soul ties, and even how God's grace can help break unhealthy bonds to other people.

After we finally said our goodbyes for the night, I knew that it wasn't an accident that we met and that there was a divine purpose for having her in my life. I had no idea just how big that purpose would be. That night, I fell on my knees, thanking God for guiding me through the day and asking Him for wisdom for the lunch date I had with Sophia the next day.

*   *   *

Weekend lunchtimes at the hostel were always special, mostly because the weekend menu was prepared by hotel chefs. The dining room always buzzed with relaxed students, using the time to catch up with friends. For me, this weekend lunchtime was special for a different reason. I made a beeline for the same table we sat at the night before, waiting excitedly for her to arrive.

Then I saw her. She approached me dressed in a white cotton shirt and a long brown skirt, smiling at me from a distance.

"How are you today? Did you sleep well? I hope I didn't trouble you much yesterday." She said upon arrival.

"Not at all! It was a pleasure to share my journey with you," I replied with a smile. I could see she was amused.

"You certainly have a way with words."

"Thank you," I said humbly, "But it's all by God's grace. All good speakers were once bad speakers! And you are very gifted too. There's something about you that makes people feel comfortable in your company, enough to pour their heart out to you."

Conversation flowed naturally from there. We talked about how our world was full of people who lied or hid the inner parts of themselves to protect themselves, putting on a mask. I told her about all the psychology material I came across, Maslow's Hierarchy of needs and everything else I learned. Sophia was intrigued, encouraging me to share it at seminars and maybe write a book. But I pointed out to her that I learned it all to help people, not for my own success.

We talked about loneliness and recovering when our relationships breakdown. We even talked about how we mourn relationships in a similar way to how we mourn a death. In both cases, we've lost someone significant from our lives, and it's easy to despair. This was clearly a poignant subject for her, and I noticed that once or twice her eyes glistened. I, too, had been there. And I knew there was life beyond loneliness.

"We can get involved in the community, investing in things bigger than ourselves. We can be intentional with our time and careful about who we spend it with," I said, calling on all my study into this very topic. We talked more about how we perceive weakness and strength in others, and how strength is so often a mask hiding fear, of one sort or another. "But," I assured her, "the Christian message is that we should be true to ourselves and others, which breaks those shackles of fear. It allows us to live in freedom and hope."

Sophia nodded, but then she asked, "Why couldn't God just create a world without pain?"

"Because we can't truly love each other or God unless we have the free will to not love," I replied.

We talked more about how God redeems us through Jesus, and how this shows how great His love is for us. I discovered she was brought up in a Greek Orthodox Church and had never seen God the way I was describing Him. She was fascinated when I said that God is good all the time, giving us access to Him through prayer. I told her about the gift of the Holy Spirit and the reasons to hope when the world turns against us. How He will never leave us or forsake us.

"I would like to pray together for my mother," she said.

I was touched by her trust in me, and so happy to see how excited she was at the idea of getting closer to God. We prayed together for a moment. Her face split into a gentle smile as she looked at me.

"Thank you!" she said at the end of our lunch together. "Can I book you in for more sessions?" We both laughed.

"I would love that." I said with a smile. I liked her determination and persistence. She was eager to learn, and I admired that. As I looked at her, something compelled me to ask her a question.

"Before you go, what would be the greatest gift you'd want from God?" She paused for a brief moment, contemplating her answer.

"Let me think about it and I'll let you know."

*　　*　　*

The next day, we met after breakfast in the prayer room. Together we prayed again for her mother, who was suffering from depression, and it was taking a toll on her body. I prayed aloud, thanking Him for this opportunity and for the healing and protection for her mother and father. I prayed that God might touch Sophia's broken heart and fill it with peace and joy. I could see that she was touched, tears flowing freely down her face, but I could also see a new glow that wasn't there before. I thanked God for this time and the heartwarming experience we got to share.

Afterward we talked quite a bit more about the nature of free will and the pressures of society. I talked more about my own background and how I witnessed miracles.

"But how did you start questioning all of this?" she asked me at one point. I quoted Matthew 7:7: "Ask and it will be given to you; seek and you will find; knock and the door will be opened to you.

"In my journey," I explained further, "I found how important it was to understand the difference between being religious and having a genuine relationship with God. Most faiths are about people trying to achieve a level with God. Christianity is about God reaching out to humanity."

"I've really enjoyed hearing your story, Sanjay," said Sophia, "I know a lot of people in the hostel, especially young girls, that I think would benefit from what you know. Would you be open to offering some guidance and counselling?"

I was flattered, but also excited by the idea. So we started planning regular group counselling sessions where people were welcome to share their problems. With Sophia, I had found my ministry. My ministry was the hostel itself. Eventually, I also started a group where people joined the prayer meeting officiated by the hostel chaplain.

At the end of the first group counselling session, Sophia confided in me that her father was once a spiritual medium and her mother always visited a fortune teller. She told me that a generational curse that afflicted the women in her family with a health problem that required medication to manage. She had grown up with doctors constantly poking and prodding her body, which she hated. It was scary, humiliating and painful.

It was difficult to tell her that her parents were involved in occult practices but she was surprisingly sanguine. I told her that dealing with the occult opens the door for the devil to enter, cursing people as he does. No matter how innocent the intention is, the possible demonic infestation is not worth the risk. I suggested that we pray for her and her family for God to forgive, cleanse, and free them from any demonic oppression. She happily joined me, and after we prayed, she told me she felt touched and blessed. I suggested she destroy any occult objects in her home, like amulets or talismans. Sophia felt gratified that there was something concrete she could do for her parents.

We started planning our next steps to help others with their problems.

*　　*　　*

With Sophia by my side, more and more girls came to visit us, sharing their problems. I met quite a few of her friends, too and found that most of the problems were about relationships, money, emotional and mental wellbeing. People were addicted to internet chat rooms and pornography, using them as an outlet to escape the stress of studies.

There was heaps of pressure on everyone to do exceptionally well at school, find a partner, and be popular. I loved listening to them as they poured their hearts out, knowing that they just wanted someone to listen. Again, I was reminded why God allowed me to go through so many isolating experiences—for moments like these, acting as His vessel and supporting His children in the hostel.

Sophia and I worked together to plan new group discussions, debates, and prayer meetings at the hostel. Eventually, I was asked to be the hostel's Sunday service speaker. When Christmas rolled around, we organised a production that displayed a range of creative performances. We showcased art, music, dance, and drama. It was a lot of work, but the whole hostel banded together like a family and made it happen. It was very gratifying to see everyone working as one.

Everything was going so well until one day, we got the news that the hostel was being sold and we all had to move to a new location. We were shocked. We couldn't imagine leaving a place we had grown to call home. We tried talking to management, but there was nothing we could do to stop it. They assured us that the new hostel would be a better place, and we should make room for change. But, like all change, it was difficult to embrace.

The new place was part hostel, part hotel. There were new people in management, and they had a different approach from what we were used to. They didn't have the same empathy and compassion; to them, the hostel was just a business.

During lunch one day, I overheard a group of the new boys pointing to a very young woman working in the kitchen. They were saying that she was an easy target and were planning on hitting on her. I glanced at the girl and noticed she was very young and innocent. I couldn't stand for it. I later approached her to warn her about the boys who wanted to take advantage of her. When I asked her for her name, my heart melted when I heard the most childish voice escape her lips.

"My name is Kristine. I'm from Indonesia." She said, shyly.

She seemed so vulnerable, and I felt a connection with her straight away. I wanted to protect her. Her English wasn't great, and she was shy. She told me she was just 15, new to London and alone. I found out that her parents had sent her to New Zealand to study when she was just 13, but that it hadn't worked out. So they arranged for her to go to London instead.

Her English hadn't been good enough for the school, so she left and was working to support herself at this young age.

I warned her about the boys, telling her to be careful, and I invited her to our fellowship group and prayer meetings. I did what I always did when I approached new people. In the moment, Kristine was just another lost soul I wanted to reach. I had no idea how important she would be in my life.

*   *   *

Kristine came to prayer groups regularly, and I loved watching her confidence grow. She didn't speak much and was very observant. She spent most of the meetings sitting and listening, not saying a single world. She only spoke when she was with just Sophia and myself. I usually only got a nod, a smile, or a heavily accented "nice". She was always the last person to leave a group session, helping us tidy up. I quickly developed a soft spot for her.

Kristine really liked to eat. I realised it was because she had experienced a lot of loneliness in New Zealand. She used to live in a room with a cruel landlady who only gave her two meals a day, usually of cheap mashed potatoes and sausages. When I heard this, it was no surprise she found something as simple as the hostel food heavenly. I never really cooked much before, but I had to learn in London and was beginning to get better. I used this newfound skill to cook for her, and anyone else who was hungry.

Kristine showed how wonderfully different she was. She always made sure I ate while the others just went ahead and had their fill. I loved her like a daughter and wanted the best for this amazing child. I helped put her through language school and coached her in her studies where I could.

Sanjay Gupta

After a few months, we had developed a strong bond, like father and daughter or older brother and younger sister. I told her to ask her father to send me a letter of authority to become her legal guardian. This would allow me to continue to help her with her schooling and access other resources to give her the best opportunities possible in the circumstances.

* * *

Dr Jonathan's home group was still going strong. I was still a consistent member and was still helping Holy Trinity's Alpha course. Soon, the hostel's management heard about my involvement and decided to run their own Alpha course, giving me full responsibility. Meetings were often at capacity, and it was a success for the hostel. Everything was going well, and God was using me in mighty ways.

But it was temporary. Out of the blue, the new management of the hostel changed the rules. Anyone aged 16 and under was no longer permitted to stay in the hostel, and within days, they issued eviction notices. Our little community was thrown into chaos. The affected students were given so little notice, it was impossible to find suitable accommodation in time, especially in central London. People were crying and had no one to turn to. I was trying my best to comfort them, helping find alternative accommodation.

My heart broke when Kristine came to me, crying. She had been given the eviction notice, too. She had two weeks to leave. I couldn't bear to see a child treated this way, a child who was alone in such big city. Luckily I had guardianship at this point, so over the next week, I worked hard for her, trying to get her a spot at almost every hostel in central London. But it was the middle of the term, and everywhere I inquired either had no vacancy or needed six months' notice to consider. In my

218

desperation, I decided to speak to our own hostel's management, trying to pull any compassion out of them so that I could at least get more time to find accommodation.

I talked to the person in charge the next morning. Surely, he would see how unreasonable it was to expect these kids to leave in two weeks. To my surprise and horror, he looked at me with loathing and condescension, asking who I was to speak on behalf of the kids. He rudely told me to mind my own business, and I realised I may as well be talking to a stone wall. The man had no compassion in him, or manners. I decided to try and get in touch with someone higher up. I was fuming inside, burning with a rage that was not going to be put out easily.

That evening, when I returned to my room, I noticed a letter. I was confused. I opened it and was shocked to find a notice asking me to vacate the premises in two weeks. I had no options. My aunt and uncle were still away, and I had limited connections in London myself. I didn't know what to do. I felt terribly helpless, powerless, and confused. Everyone was looking up to me for hope and support, but I was at a complete loss of what to do next.

Tired and exhausted, I locked myself in my room, fell on my knees and prayed.

"God, I don't know what to do. You know the situation. I see no way out, please help me." I fell on the floor and cried. *I will never leave you nor forsake you, and all things work for the good of those who love Him.* God's promise rang in my mind again. God spoke to me through the Bible, Psalm 91.

He who dwells in the secret place of the Most High
Shall abide under the shadow of the Almighty.
I will say of the Lord, "He is my refuge and my fortress;

My God, in Him I will trust."

Surely He shall deliver you from the snare of the fowler

And from the perilous pestilence.

He shall cover you with His feathers,

And under His wings you shall take refuge;

His truth shall be your shield and buckler.

You shall not be afraid of the terror by night,

Nor of the arrow that flies by day,

Nor of the pestilence that walks in darkness,

Nor of the destruction that lays waste at noonday.

A thousand may fall at your side,

And ten thousand at your right hand;

But it shall not come near you.

Only with your eyes shall you look,

And see the reward of the wicked.

Because you have made the Lord, who is my refuge,

Even the Most High, your dwelling place,

No evil shall befall you,

Nor shall any plague come near your dwelling;

For He shall give His angels charge over you,

To keep you in all your ways.

In their hands they shall bear you up,

Lest you dash your foot against a stone.

You shall tread upon the lion and the cobra,

The young lion and the serpent you shall trample underfoot.

Because he has set his love upon Me, therefore I will deliver him;

I will set him on high, because he has known My name.

He shall call upon Me, and I will answer him;

I will be with him in trouble;

I will deliver him and honour him.
With long life I will satisfy him,
And show him My salvation.

God had moved again. I felt a supernatural level of peace come over me, and soon enough God brought all my loved ones to help and support me. Phonsie drove me 70 miles to meet the head of the hostel only to be told that the situation was out of his hands. Jonathan and the home group prayed for me constantly for protection and peace. Ps David Hurst connected me to his lawyer friend to help me get an injunction against the eviction notice, completely free of charge. Ps David also told me that God gave him a vision for me while he was praying and that I would have a very big house where I would be able to bless a lot of people. I could only hope! The other students even wrote letters on my behalf to the management, telling them about my contribution to the residents.

The management got calls from most of the home group members and, finally, after the injunction came through, chose to meet with me and discuss what was going to happen. I told them that all I needed was enough time to find new accommodation and move into the new place smoothly. They agreed, mostly because the court was twisting their arm.

After a very chaotic week, God came through with another victory. I found a house, just five minutes away from the hostel. It was huge, and with the help and support of Sophia, we moved in with Kristine and two other girls. It was hard for us to rebuild our lives yet again, but step by step, we managed. I found myself taking care of a family I truly loved. It was a whole new level of richness and fulfilment. I was reminded of the Romans 8:28: All things work for the good of those who love Him.

This whole incident taught me a lot about spiritual battles. I knew better than ever to love the sinner and hate the sin. I found a new level of dependence on God when I had seen so many times how he provided for me. Prayer had real power; I knew it not just because I had seen it, but because I had that faith. As time went on, I saw more and more miracles in my life and in the lives of the people around me, confirming again and again just how great God is.

*   *   *

In the midst of all these changes, my job with Stephen's company came to an end as well. The business had been a good one, but had fallen on hard time. I was out of work. Sophia was of great moral support during this time. She prayed with me to help me find a new path. She typed a CV for me and suggested I go to the Job Centre to see what God had in store for me.

One day, I got all my paperwork together and went to the Oxford Street Job Centre to have a look. I quickly discovered there was nothing available. As I was leaving the centre, very disappointed, my eyes fell on an advertisement: "Great communication skills required." It was a customer service job for a rail company. I went back into the counter to ask about it.

I was told that 700 people had already applied for that one post. I decided to go for it anyway. I was given a multipage form to fill in, and it was the closing day for the applications. I didn't know what else to do, so I prayed, stapled my CV with the form, and posted it.

Two weeks later I was called for the test and the interview. I got the job working for one of the greatest rail company that gave me the most exciting, rewarding, and enriching experiences.

*   *   *

At the beginning of my spiritual journey, the first time I heard a sermon from the pulpit, I noted down seven promises of God. Reflecting on my life, I revisited these notes and saw that each of these promises came true. He never left nor forsook me, He cleansed me of my sin, built me up, comforted me, communicated with me, made me a fisher of men, and came again. While the last one has been in a spiritual sense rather than the physical return of Christ, I can attest to his faithfulness and how He came back for me again and again. He has provided my finances, friends, and courses, and has continually healed my heart, soul, mind, and body. Life was imperfect, but in my moments of heartbreak, God comforted me.

A few years after moving into the new house we had constant problems with our greedy and ruthless landlord. Once he threatened to evict us unless we paid more. I felt as if I was in a battle and my heart was in agony at the thought of losing our home. He always mocked my faith in God and claimed that there was no heaven or hell but everything in life was about money. According to him, money was the only god. He was married thrice and all his three wives were dead. I would pray for him daily, but I found myself wondering if I could meet someone who had seen heaven and hell. Around this time I read about a man named Ian McCormack who had been declared dead for 15 minutes after being stung by five box jellyfish. I first heard him speak at a service and eventually became friends with him.

He was the first person in my life who talked about what heaven and hell looked like and his experience with a glimpse of eternity after death. He wasn't Christian when he was stung by the jellyfish. He told the congregation that hell was like waking up in the middle of the night, trying to find a light switch but never reaching it. No matter how much he moved, he was completely surrounded by a darkness so thick, he couldn't see his hand in front of his face. He knew that he was, in that moment, a spiritual being with no physical body.

Goosebumps danced on my arms as I listened to his story. He said he felt an intense coldness and fear enveloping him, as if someone was staring at him in the darkness but he couldn't see who it was. Slowly, he became overly aware that there were other people moving around him, just as lost and confused and scared.

Heaven he described as a brilliant light that drew him out of the darkness. He was amazed by the brilliance of it all. He felt weightless, the light shifting the heavy darkness and fear off him.

"I didn't want to look back too much in case I fell back into the darkness," he said. His face broke into a look of pure joy as he described the light. It was as if the light was alive, emanating a peace that he never found on earth. I was on the edge of my seat as he said he believed that what he saw was the glory of God. He felt absolute love and power in that moment, knowing that whoever was radiating it must be the King of Kings and the Lord of Lords.

There was an altar call at the end of his sermon, and, in a hall of around 500 people, over 100 responded, asking for prayer. I was standing in the third row, lost in the crowd. So I was amazed when he came down, walking directly to me. He put his hand on my heart and prayed.

"God heal this man's broken heart for he is hurting," he began. "Touch him this evening, Lord. Thank you for this brother. Take his pain away, master. Bless him Lord in abundance. In Jesus' name, Amen."

I met Ian a couple of times after that and got to know him on a personal level. I asked him how he knows who to pray for. He said simply that God guides and speaks to him in his heart.

* * *

One day, Sophia asked me how I would know what God wanted me to do, and I told her that I trusted He would create a situation to send me a message. Barely five minutes after I said this, the phone rang. It was a member from Jonathan's home group. She was an administrator on a radio station who had been asking me for a while now to speak on the talk show, Dawn Traders. It was a platform for business and traders to discuss different issues that they struggled with. I wasn't keen when she called me this time, either, but she told me Jonathan would be speaking too and I would be accompanying him. It sounded like a great idea. We had no idea what to expect, we were just excited for the opportunity.

It was 4.55 on a Saturday morning when Jonathan and I entered the radio station. We were introduced to the crew and were shown to the studio where the microphones were set up. Jonathan had just started speaking about prayer and worship when dozens of calls came through. They hurled abuse, using filthy crude words to insult him. It was clear from the outset that they were against the Christian faith. Jonathan was pretty shaken, so I decided to take over.

I asked the callers what their problem was and heard one of them say we were stupid to talk about God when there was so much evil in the world. He mentioned wars, disease, natural disasters, and hunger. He asked why God didn't do anything about them. At this point, I was used to this way of thinking and knew how to handle the man. I explained that humans—not God—created scarcity through greed and hubris, and that this is what drove the evils he had listed.

I went on to refute every other question the callers threw at us. The listeners were furious, asking me to come back again so they could continue the argument. It went for weeks, and I was in high demand, albeit not for the best reasons. It got to a point where the listeners would choose a topic during the week for me to talk on each Saturday morning. The show became increasingly popular, and I ended up speaking there for over 18 months. I covered a variety of topics including phobias, relationships, Hinduism, and cults. The topics changed every week so I always had something new to talk about and share.

Soon, my popularity grew, not just as a target to question, but personally. I had regular fans who were actually keen to hear me speak every week. I got calls from politicians, religious and social groups, as well as other radio and TV stations. I was even blessed with the opportunity to interview four candidates running for Mayor of London. I was once invited for lunch to the Neasden Hindu Temple to meet the high priests there. A popular Asian newspaper asked me to write a column, and people kept asking if I had a book.

On principle, I refrained from meeting my listeners in public. I didn't want to be idolized, nor did I want to send the wrong message to people. There were a few with whom I chose to meet up who needed serious help or guidance.

One of my listeners was a lady who helped manage an Islamic television channel. She kept asking if I would like be a guest on her show, which I always declined. Television felt like too much exposure. But, I soon got a call from the TV station saying the channel was holding a religious debate, and I was invited to speak with Islamic preachers. It seemed like God was creating another opportunity for me to share my views.

The night before the show, I fasted and prayed, telling God I was going in, not by my own strength, but by his power. I was giving all glory to Him. I arrived at the TV station, ready for the debate. But none of the other speakers showed up. The producers were getting desperate. It was almost time for them to go live, and still there was no one. They asked me if I would be willing to go live alone. I could feel their doubt as they made the request but knew they had no other option.

One of the presenters asked me to give her a list of questions they could ask me, clearly unsure that I would be able to answer questions any other way. I told her she could interrogate me any way she liked. My only request was that I wanted to describe the difference between faith, religion, and relationship. She hesitantly agreed and the show began.

It was supposed to go for two hours, starting with my introduction and a brief summary of my spiritual journey. I explained that humanity is born into a religion but that does not necessarily mean that we have a relationship with God. I delved into the faith-religion-relationship dynamic, and we immediately received dozens of calls. People were giving their input and expressing their understanding of religion. I talked about my journey from Hinduism to atheism and, finally, my leap into finding a personal relationship with Christ.

I was asked why I chose Christ, and I told them," My relationship with Christ had transformed me."

After 44 minutes, the show was cut short. I was confused but I later discovered that some viewers were not happy that a non-Muslim was holding his own against the presenters of the show. They were sending threats. One of the technicians told me that they were more accustomed to guests from outside religions speaking nervously.

"But you," he said, incredulous, "are the first person I have seen that has shaken all of us."

To me, that was a success, and I thanked God for the victory. The producer was very pleased with my performance and asked if I would do a show called Hard Talk. Though the offer was tempting, I wasn't ready for it and politely declined. All of the tough times in my life had culminated in moments like this. God had allowed me to go through it all to educate me so I could, in turn, educate others.

From this moment on, God filled my life with so many different kinds of people. I encountered all kinds of struggles and had the opportunity to pray for so many people, having the privilege to witness His healing and miracles.

*   *   *

One day, I was talking to Sophia and I remembered one of the first questions I asked her when we met. What would be the greatest gift God could give her? I hadn't received an answer yet. She looked at me thoughtfully and confided that the best gift she could receive was for the generational curse upon her family to be broken. She wanted the women in her family to be healed and restored so that they didn't have to rely on medication for their health.

The next Sunday evening, we went to Holy Trinity Brompton, and after the service, we kneeled down and prayed. I asked for healing in Jesus' name to invade her world, believing in complete restoration for her, her mother, and all the women in her family who were affected. In exactly 28 days, she was completely healed, and her mother's worry about it came to an end.

Her mother was so thankful that she sent me a gold crown which she had kept as an offering for her church if Sophia was healed. I told Sophia to take the crown back since I wasn't the one who healed her. It was all God. Our Healer gave the gift for free. I did, however, meet Sophia's mother, who spent a lot of time asking me questions about life. I was happy with how life was going.

One of the biggest miracles in my life came not long after. I got a call from Calcutta. My mother was very ill and in hospital. She was going to die. The doctors had given up all hope, and they wanted me to come as soon as possible to say goodbye. I loved my mother very much and couldn't bear the idea of losing her. There had to be something we could do.

I know my God is a God of miracles, so I did the only thing I could think of in that moment. I called a Christian friend of mine in Calcutta, Jimmy, to visit my mother in hospital and pray for her. I asked him to give the phone to her so that I could speak to her. I told her that I loved her. And then I told her that the one person that could save her was Jesus and that she should invite Him into her life.

I held my breath, waiting for a response. By God's grace, my mother invited Jesus into her life. I was overwhelmed with joy, happy tears running down my face. She grew stronger and began to recover her health. I arranged with relatives to fly her out to London, so I could be with her. When she arrived, I took care of her with the help of some of the members at my local church, and she soon was on the road to recover. The power of the almighty God, our Lord and Saviour was so evident in her. God has healed so many people with seemingly incurable diseases right in front of my eyes, including injuries to my own body. God is truly a God of miracles.

*   *   *

When Kristine was a little older, I wanted to put her in one of the best high schools in London, but even pooling our resources, Sophia and I didn't have that kind of money. The cost of the school was £12000 a year, but we could only manage £5000. I really wanted her to study in that school so I kept praying, knowing God would come through for me.

In the meantime, Kristine had registered herself at another, cheaper school in a neighbourhood that didn't have the best reputation. It was her last day of secondary school, and she was going to say goodbye to her school friends before paying the money in full to her new high school. I still hadn't given up praying all throughout that afternoon. When I got home, I found a letter from the more expensive high school lying on my doormat.

It had been such long time since I applied for an online brochure, and it had finally come. I called the school immediately and asked about it. The secretary of the school answered, and I was surprised when she told me that I had an appointment with the principal that afternoon. I couldn't believe it. I told her I would definitely be there, barely able to contain my excitement. I had to get Kristine.

I tried calling her, but her phone was off. I left three messages, telling her to come home and to see me before she went anywhere else. Finally, half an hour before our appointment, Kristine returned home. And then it was a rush from there. I quickly explained to her that I was going to ask the principal to take her for £5000. Kristine looked at me in disbelief, saying it would be impossible, there was no point in trying.

But there was also no harm in trying. And even if it made no logical sense to offer less than half the tuition, I knew my God was bigger than logic.

We reached the school and spoke to the secretary who directed us to the waiting room while she informed the principal of our arrival. My heart was beating hard and fast as we waited. After about a minute, the principal came out and invited us to his office. From the beginning of the meeting, I was direct and upfront.

"Sir," I began, confidently, "this is Kristine. She is a part of my family here in London and is very precious and dear to me. I want the very best for her, and I chose this school because it offers the best. Unfortunately, Kristine's parents are in Indonesia and have been going through quite a few hardships. All we can offer is £5000. I don't want to waste your time but if there is any provision for people in extreme circumstances in your school, then I'm happy to discuss that further with you. Otherwise, we shall take our leave."

The principal was motionless for a moment, studying Kristine and myself, processing what I had just told him.

With a deep sigh, he said, "Give me five minutes to speak to someone, and I'll get back to you."

Those five minutes were some of the most nerve-wracking minutes in my life. It was as though all the feelings of trepidation before sitting an exam and getting the results had all combined into one. After what felt like an eternity, the principal returned, holding a few papers.

"You can fill in this form and register her with just £100 now," He began. "Then you can pay the full amount later. We have accepted her with the £5000 you've offered."

I was speechless. I was trying to thank him, but my throat was dry. Eventually, I gathered the words to show my appreciation and thanked God for the wonderful miracle.

*   *   *

As I reflect on my life now, I can't help but smile as I remember each and every miracle, even before I had a real relationship with God. After Kristine's acceptance to school, I started thinking about how all of this began, and I quickly discovered just how early God had been working in my life.

An acquaintance, Sister Jane, came over for dinner. She was a senior member of an African church and very active in the community. After dinner, she was praying for my mother and asked her when she first started going to church. She was fascinated to hear that my mother was from a Hindu background yet knew so much about the Christian faith. I was curious to hear what my mother was going to say to this, and I was surprised at her answer.

"I've been going to church since even before Sanjay was born. There's a church just across from our house, and every time the church bell rang, I felt like God was calling me, and I would go and sit there in His presence. Sanjay was a little baby when I carried him to the church, put him at the altar and prayed. I prayed to our Heavenly Father. I remember saying to Him, 'I know my baby's earthly father is not capable of taking care of him, so I surrender him to You. Take care of my baby.' And God has done exactly that. He has taken care of Him ever since."

My heart skipped a beat when I heard this. I moved to another room, fell to my knees and cried. God has been so faithful. He had been honouring my mother's prayers from the beginning, protecting and guiding me throughout my life. He never let me go, even when I was lonely, hurting, confused, even contemplating suicide. He had been my shepherd, my friend, my guide, and above all, my Saviour. I was having a very real revelation about the reality of Psalm 23: The Lord is my shepherd; I shall not want. All things work for good for those who love Him.

A few days later, I was in David Hurst's Pastorate, listening to a new speaker who was born again from a Hindu background. He was sharing his testimony, speaking wonderfully to the congregation when he suddenly turned to me.

"Brother, there is a book in you that needs to get out in the world. You have been holding on to it for too long. The time is now."

He prayed for me afterwards, and I was stunned that God had spoken to me so clearly. But how could I still be surprised? God always has His ways. I invited the speaker to our house a couple of weeks later and had great fellowship with Ps David.

I didn't know how or where to start with the book. I prayed and prayed, asking God for guidance, and finally, I have been able to put this book together. My journey for finding the truth has led me to a number of conclusions. I started with what I thought were unanswerable questions, sure that faith was ridiculous. And now, my journey has brought me here. In love with God and serving Him with all that I have.

God has created us all as a masterpiece. He has given us everything we need in life, to do the works he has planned for us. He wants to transform our lives through faith and miracles, not by religious rituals. When we accept Jesus Christ as our Saviour, the Holy Spirit resides within us. He offers hope, and it is never too late to restore your heart to Him.

Spiritual growth is a lifelong process, and everyone's path is takes a different route and speed. Our focus should not be on each other, but on our own faith and relationship with God.

When all doors are shut, God will open another. He can transform any ordinary or hopeless situation into an extraordinary one. Even ordinary and hopeless Sanjay can be transformed into someone extraordinary to whom others look for support, guidance, and protection.

God's love is unconditional and He cares for us so much that He is always ready to crown us with glory and honour, even in the presence of our enemies. So while I will never stop learning, the questions that plagued me at the beginning of my journey are now answered.

I had thought that the greatest power a man can have is the control of other people's minds. But now I knew that our true power is putting our entire faith in the even greater power of God.

The greatest desire a man can have is not to be God, but the yearning for divine love and healing from God, His Son, and the Holy Spirit.

And the greatest treasures a man can have is freedom of thoughts and expression, and delivery from sin and death.

In my journey for truth, I have found that God had kept me in His will, mercy, and grace and never left me alone, ever. My heart is filled with gratitude that he gave me wisdom and courage to share my journey with you. Having a personal relationship with Him, I am more convinced than ever that Jesus Christ is exactly who he claims to be: the Way, the Truth, and the Life. God has filled my life with joy and blessings. He has used me to touch the lives of so many people. He is the beginning and the end, the alpha and the omega.

I have discovered again and again: A book can inform you, a seminar can reform you but a relationship with Jesus Christ will transform you.

God bless.

Epilogue

So much has happened since that moment, but to write about it all would take me another volume. God has place a burden in my heart to reach people, especially the true seekers who are duped by false religions and prophets. I live by faith and the way God leads me.

Pursuing my quest for public speaking has opened many doors to speak in the UK and other parts of Europe. I have interacted with spiritually hungry people from all walks of life and from all over the world seeking truth.

I have also met scores of people like me who escaped from darkness into true light by the Grace of God, and I have witnessed great healing and miracles.

I thank God for taking me out of darkness and using me in a mighty way to touch the lives of people.

ABOUT THE AUTHOR

Sanjay Gupta is a professional speaker and has trained hundreds of people from all over the world in Spoken English, Public Speaking, Body language, Personal development and Effective Communication. He has been awarded the Performers Certificate from the Trinity College of London in Effective Communication. He has been a motivational speaker on the radio in London. He has won numerous speaking competitions in both Toastmasters UK and The Association of Public Speakers UK. He was in the Toastmasters 2014 Humorous speech UK national competition. He has been part of a great rail company for the past 19 years.

He lives in London and helps out in a number of charitable organisations